The little bell tinkled alerting me that someone had walked into my store.

Delighted, I hurried back out to stand behind the counter.

A handsome man stood there, just inside the door, looking around.

All in black, he was wearing a long wool coat, leather gloves, and a warm cap. He held a red shopping bag in one hand.

"Hello," I said, with a smile. "Welcome."

"Hi," he said, looking at me with a rather perplexed expression.

"What are you looking for?"

"I'm not sure," he said, his gaze flicking over in the direction of the Christmas tree.

"Is it for a Christmas gift?"

He turned and looked into my eyes.

"A wedding gift," he said. "For my sister."

I grinned. "She's getting married? That's wonderful. When?"

"Christmas Eve," he said.

"That's exciting," I said. "What a wonderful day to get married. It's my favorite day in the whole year."

He just looked at me.

"Do you want help or do you just want to look around?" I asked.

I honestly had not expected my first customer to be a man. I didn't know much about how men shopped, except for my brother Colton. And I'd only seen him buy things like flour at the General Store.

"I don't know yet," he said. "I guess I'll look around some."

"Okay." I smiled and sat down on my stool. I rested my elbows on the counter and my chin on my hands to watch him.

He walked over to the tree and lightly touched one of the red ribbons.

"You're my first customer," I said, standing up and smiling broadly.

TWILIGHT FROST

TWILIGHT FROST

THE BECQUERELS

KATHRYN KALEIGH

To learn more about Kathryn Kaleigh, visit

www.kathrynkaleigh.com

Kathryn Kaleigh

PROLOGUE

*E*very Christmas Eve at twilight a ghost appeared in front of the old Colorado blue spruce in Auclair Memorial Park.

Not just any ghost, but the ghost of Elise Auclair.

No one ever questioned that it was Elise.

According to the legend of Whiskey Springs, Elise waited there for her one true love.

They made a promise to meet there, but he never returned.

So she came back every year. Year after year.

Waiting…

1

BENJAMIN SMITH

Today

"You have got to be—" I bit my tongue. "A week?"

In my eight years as a pilot, I had never once had a flat tire on an airplane.

Until today.

After grabbing a quick hamburger at the edge of town, I'd come back to the airport, a generous term for what was little more than a runway, just outside the small mountain town of Whiskey Springs to run through my preflight checklist and do a walk around.

A flat tire.

Normally a flat tire would be no problem. But here at this airport they had no way to fix a flat. No replacement tires or even the right kind of valve for me to fix it myself.

So I had to wait. A winter snow storm was keeping any kind of courier from getting through. It didn't help that the holidays were here.

I called everywhere and everyone I knew who might have any kind of solution.

Opening my iPad, I checked the weather. Snow. And not just snow. Heavy snow.

A winter storm warning.

This storm had not been in the forecast.

Maybe on one of the obscure ones that I checked on occasion, but not the National Weather Service. Not on NOAA.

A freak snow storm, they were calling it.

And I just happened to be sitting here with a flat tire.

Less than one week until Christmas. My sister's wedding in Houston. On Christmas Eve.

I gave some serious thought to flying anyway. Knelt down on the tarmac and ran my hand along the deflated nitrogen tire. I was certain it was the valve stem, but there was a puncture hole near it, too.

Standing up, I looked toward the mountain peaks, snow clouds clustered around them. Definitely snow in the high country.

The wind, much stronger than it had been when I had landed, whipped at my coat. Definitely stronger than it had been just over an hour ago. I pulled off my hat and tossed it inside the cockpit then climbed inside.

My mentor, Noah Worthington, had drilled safety into my head above all else. *A reckless pilot is a dead pilot* he would say.

I made the phone calls I needed to make. Ordered what I needed to order. When the weather cleared my tire would be on the way. Then I got to work busy finding myself a place to stay.

All the major hotels were booked. The weather, of course. And on top of that it was a week before Christmas.

Everyone recommended the Auclair House, a bed and breakfast on the north side of town.

Unable to find anything online about it, I called the number the guy at the Holiday Inn gave me.

The young lady who answered the phone claimed to have one room left. I made a reservation with my credit card, called an Uber, and headed in that direction.

The Uber driver was chatty. Although I wasn't in the mood, I heard every word he said.

"That's the Whiskey Springs Saloon," he said. "Started the whole town right there. It was a boarding house, an entertainment house, and a saloon all at the same time."

It looked rather small to have served all those purposes, but it had a fresh coat of paint and some plate glass windows that obviously had been added later. It had obviously been taken care of over the years.

It was dead center in the middle of town, so it looked like the town had spread out around it, like he said.

"On the left over there is the park. It's only been a park for about a hundred years or so give or take a few decades. It started off as one of Bailey Auclair's favorite places to come and paint."

"Who's that?" I asked when he took a breath.

"Famous artist. You're not from here," he said, not even pausing for confirmation. "That Colorado blue spruce has been there for probably eight hundred years."

"Looks like it," I said under my breath, but he heard me and sent me a look.

"It's a short walk from the park—The Auclair Memorial Park—to the Auclair Bed and Breakfast where you'll be staying. You should walk down there. Most folks appreciate it."

"The Auclairs are a big name around here."

"They weren't the first ones here, but they made their place here in town, as well as having property on the other side of the park."

"Impressive," I said, a little curious in spite of myself about this Auclair family.

"You'll see their name alongside Dr. Alexander Avery's. He was a major founder of the town."

"What did the Auclairs do?" I asked.

"Only two of them ended up staying in town," he said. "For different reasons. The girl stayed the longest."

He stopped the car at the curb in front of a rather large two-story house that was definitely old. I preferred the modern conveniences of hotels over the older bed and breakfasts. Room service. Televisions. Plenty of hot water.

"We're here," the driver said. "Told you it wasn't far from the park."

I only had a small overnight bag with me. The one I always kept in the plane with me. Just in case. Didn't have any winter clothes in there though, so I was going to be making a shopping trip downtown tonight or in the morning.

Fortunately it was a short walk to town so I could easily avoid having to call a driver.

"Doesn't look like much on the outside," the driver said. "But it's nice on the inside. Been kept up to date." Seems the Uber driver was a mind reader, too.

Now that I was here I started thinking just how nice it was going to be to have a few days to myself. I had a lot of alone time to think in the cockpit, but being able to walk around, look at different things, that was long overdue.

There was only one definite downside. I had to call my sister. Let her know I wasn't going to make it to her wedding.

I'd never tell her, but there were worse things than missing a wedding with two thousand guests. Maybe not two thousand, but might as well be. I seriously doubted she'd even miss me other than maybe at picture taking time.

The Uber driver had told me the truth. The inside of the house was elegantly furnished. Decked out in Christmas colors of crimson and silver. A huge fir tree took up one quadrant of the living room that served as a lobby, festively lit with thousands of clear twinkling lights. Red and silver wax coated pine cones. And glass balls of all sorts.

I wondered what was up with the wax coated pine cones.

"Mr. Smith," the girl I had talked to behind the counter greeted me.

I nodded.

"Welcome to the Auclair Bed and Breakfast." She smiled. She was most definitely not from here. She had a southern accent that I could spot a mile away. I had an aunt from Alabama and I would put money on her being from there. Birmingham maybe. Or Auburn.

"Do you have more luggage?" she asked.

"It was an unplanned trip," I said.

"Right. You're the pilot," she said.

"That's right," I said. "Word travels fast."

"Small town," she said, with a little shrug. "Your room is on the second floor just up the stairs and to the right. You'll have a great view of downtown from there. And if you listen on a clear night, you can hear music coming from the saloon."

"Do I need to fill anything out?"

"Nah. It's a bed and breakfast. Not a big chain hotel." She smiled. "Besides, your credit card went through so you're good."

She slid a key across the counter. "Breakfast at six. Or you can have something sent up later."

"I'll just have something sent up." After I got off the phone with my family, I was going to need some sleep.

"Just call down when you're ready for breakfast," she said. "Have a good night."

It was only four o'clock in the afternoon. As I went up the stairs decked out with flocked green garland wrapped around the bannister, the grandfather clock began to chime the hour.

Four chimes, the last one hanging in the air as I reached the second floor.

It felt like a whole lot later though, especially with the early evening darkness settling in.

I went inside my room, sprawled across the bed and kicked off my shoes.

Maybe I'd just take a nap before making my phone calls.

After about half a minute, my phone started vibrating.

With a groan, I sat up and loosened my tie.

There was a letter on my nightstand, my name scrawled across the front in a girlish handwriting.

Nice touch, I thought.

I picked up the letter. It was sealed, so I checked my phone messages first.

NICOLE: *Saw the storm on the Weather Channel. Please tell me you're on your way back to Houston.*

Might as well get the worst of it over with. Rip off the band-aid.

ME: *Bad news. Had a flat tire in Whiskey Springs. But I'm ok.*

I added that last part in there just to temper her reaction. Normally Nicole thought of others before herself, but with her wedding being in merely days, I knew that was not going to be the case.

Thought bubbles.

Since I really didn't want to know what she had to say right now, I set my phone on the nightstand, face down. It wasn't like I could do anything about it. Stranded was stranded. My family knew it was a hazard of being a private airplane pilot.

I laid back on the bed and unfolded the letter addressed to me.

DEAR BENJAMIN,
   I know you had to go. That you had no choice.

I'll just say it. Please come back.
If you believe... If you believe in us...
Meet me at the park at Twilight tonight. Christmas Eve.
I'll be there. Waiting for you.
No matter when. I'll be there.
Please don't leave me here without you.
Yours forever,
Elise

FEELING like I had intruded on someone else's personal correspondence, I quickly refolded the letter and put it back on the nightstand.

Smith was a common last name. Benjamin Smith not so much.

But this was obviously a mistake.

I would take it downstairs later. Give it to the girl behind the desk.

Let her find out who it really belonged to.

ELISE AUCLAIR

1869
Whiskey Springs

I hummed to myself as I arranged decorations in the display window.

My shop had the only display window in Whiskey Springs and I was rather proud of that fact.

My little store had only one window, to the left as you walk in the front door, so I needed lots of candles to keep things bright.

It didn't matter that my display window was little more than a window seat with a wide shelf, it was still a store front window and I treated it as such.

I decorated it with two oversized handwoven reed baskets with rope handles. One overflowing with red wax coated pinecones and the other overflowing with silver wax coated pinecones.

After backing up and studying it for a moment, I tipped the

baskets over, arranging the pinecones to look like they were spilling out.

I added a couple of books and rounded it off with a frilly straw hat I'd ordered from a dressmaker in Boston.

As for the pinecones, my sister, Bailey, had started the whole thing last Christmas during a terrible blizzard.

Her husband, an innovative man had given her the idea and Bailey had run with it.

The best part was that my little shop was the only place around here to buy the wax-coated pinecones.

Personally, I liked the two colors, red and silver, together for Christmas enough to adopt them for my own decoration theme in my own house.

The Christmas tree in one corner of my shop was festively decorated with some of those silver and red pinecones. Silver and red ribbons and bows cascading over it. And glass balls that had come from back east. Everything on the tree was for sale.

Someday we wouldn't have to order things from back east. Someday Whiskey Springs would be big enough that we would have everything we needed right here. That was, at least, my hope.

I went back behind the counter and straightened a glass jar filled with little peppermint sticks. Took one out and popped it in my mouth.

Everything looked ready for business, so I unlocked the front doors. Less than one week before Christmas. A good time for my grand opening.

Today was opening day. I was a little bit nervous, wondering how many customers I would have. Several townspeople had stopped by while I was getting everything ready and they had all been encouraging. All of them agreed that Whiskey Springs needed a shop like this.

I sat behind the counter and watched the morning traffic

outside the front of my shop. People walking here and there. Horses and buggies passing by. A stagecoach rumbled past, leaving town.

After about an hour of not having any customers, I went into the back room for a drink of water.

The shop had been merely something I wanted to do. Not something I had to do.

I'd enjoyed the planning, the shopping, the setting up.

Now it was mine.

The downside of that was that I had sunk most everything I had into it. So now I was committed.

Still, if not a single customer walked through that door, I had done what I wanted to do. And yet it had taken on an importance of its own.

As the youngest of five siblings, that had not been easy. All of my sisters and even my brother had their own ideas about how I should live my life.

Get married and have a family. That was, of course, the most popular suggestion, but it was expected of all young ladies. I wasn't going to just willy-nilly pick some man and marry him for the sake of getting married. I had my own thoughts on that one.

Start a school and teach. Whiskey Springs had no school and, granted, it would have satisfied my entrepreneurial spirit, but teaching was not my passion. Neither were children. I didn't dislike children, I just didn't necessarily like them.

Work as a seamstress and do sewing for people. Sitting alone all day sewing for people might have meaningful for any of my other sisters, but not me. I liked people. I liked having people around to talk to. That was one of the reasons I had opened this store. My three older sisters had married and moved out, leaving just me and my brother. My brother, Colton, had a wandering spirit so he was rarely home. That left me there alone.

Long ago, back when we lived in Mississippi, I'd seen a painting of a department store in London that had a lovely front display window. That image had stayed with me and I'd often imagined what it would be like to have own shop window to decorate.

The little bell tinkled alerting me that someone had walked into my store.

Delighted, I hurried back out to stand behind the counter.

A handsome man stood there, just inside the door, looking around.

All in black, he was wearing a long wool coat, leather gloves, and a warm cap. He held a red shopping bag in one hand.

"Hello," I said, with a smile. "Welcome."

"Hi," he said, looking at me with a rather perplexed expression.

"What are you looking for?"

"I'm not sure," he said, his gaze flicking over in the direction of the Christmas tree.

"Is it for a Christmas gift?"

He turned and looked into my eyes.

"A wedding gift," he said. "For my sister."

I grinned. "She's getting married? That's wonderful. When?"

"Christmas Eve," he said.

"That's exciting," I said. "What a wonderful day to get married. It's my favorite day in the whole year."

He just looked at me.

"Do you want help or do you just want to look around?" I asked.

I honestly had not expected my first customer to be a man. I didn't know much about how men shopped, except for my brother Colton. And I'd only seen him buy things like flour at the General Store.

"I don't know yet," he said. "I guess I'll look around some."

"Okay." I smiled and sat down on my stool. I rested my elbows on the counter and my chin on my hands to watch him.

He walked over to the tree and lightly touched one of the red ribbons.

"You're my first customer," I said, standing up and smiling broadly.

3

BENJAMIN

I'd decided that it would be best to go into town today since it looked like the storm would be coming in hard tonight.

I needed to get some heavy boots to wear in the snow if nothing else.

A week. It was still sinking in that I was going to have to spend a whole week here in Whiskey Springs. It wasn't that it was a bad little town. It was actually quaint and historical with a certain charm.

It was just... this was Christmas week. I would be missing all the Christmas gatherings. The office party.

My sister's wedding.

I did not mind missing the wedding. But the wrath of both my sister and my mother would come down on my head.

It wasn't even that I was all that close to my family. We all just sort of did our own thing.

"Are you new here then?" I asked. If I was her first customer, she must be new.

The girl behind the counter was young and obviously quite naïve.

"New?" she asked. "The store just opened today."

A quick gaze around told me everything did look new. Old-fashioned, but new.

"I see," I said.

It was a rather eclectic shop. Obviously designed for women. Christmas decorations—lots of those. Candles. Books.

The young lady came out from behind the counter and I blinked hard.

She was wearing a long dress. Not just long, but old-fashioned.

Old-fashioned was definitely the theme in here.

The skirts of her silver dress belled out around her. The dress had a high neckline and long sleeves. Her dark brunette hair fell loosely around her shoulders.

She had a classic heart-shaded face with smooth delicate skin and pink bow-shaped lips.

She looked just like a southern belle. It was a rather charming outfit and she wore it well.

"I have lots of Christmas decorations," she said. "But that probably wouldn't make a good wedding gift." She tapped a finger against her chin, deep in thought.

"A candle, maybe?" she suggested.

"Maybe." I was intrigued by her and had quite honestly lost interest in buying a gift for my sister, since I hadn't had a whole lot to begin with. I'd already spent a fortune buying a silverware set off her wedding registry at Williams Sonoma.

I had only ducked in here to get warm before heading back to the bed and breakfast.

"Why don't you give me a tour?" I asked.

Her face brightened. "Okay."

Deftly managing the skirts of her dress, she walked first to the Christmas tree. "All of these decorations are for sale, of course. The pinecones are all hand-dipped in red and silver wax."

"Who dipped them?" I asked.

"I did," she said, then kept going without a hitch. "There are lots of different kinds of decorations on here."

She carefully plucked one from the tree. "This is my favorite one," she said, holding it out in her palm for me to see.

I leaned close to look at it. The sparkly glass ornament had a tiny little cottage inside it. Sort of like a ship in a bottle, except it was a cottage in a ball. Sort of like a snow globe without the snow.

"This is beautiful," I said. "You made this, too?"

"No, Silly," she said, with a little laugh. "These are imported from a glass-blower on the east coast."

"It's the prettiest ornament I've ever seen." I looked at her. And she was one of the prettiest girls. She had an innocence about her and a friendly charm that could not be feigned.

"It really is," she said, looking at it again.

"I'd like to buy it," I said.

"Okay." Her smile faltered just a little. She seemed pulled between making a sale and selling her favorite ornament.

"Is this the only one like it that you have?" I asked.

"They're all hand-made one of a kind."

"You should keep it," I said.

"No, of course not," she said, smiling again. "It's for purchase. I'll wrap it up for you."

In the spirit of Christmas, I knew what I was going to do with it. I was going to give it to her.

She carefully wrapped the ornament in a velvet cloth and placed it in my hands.

"Put this in your pocket," she said.

"But I haven't paid for it."

"I'll start a tab for you," she said. "You can settle up in a bit."

"Okay," I said. "But you have to let me pay you before I leave."

"Okay. "She put her hands behind her back. "Anything else?" she asked,

"I don't know," I said. "What about the rest of my tour?"

"Oh. Of course."

I noticed there were paintings scattered on all the walls.

She walked towards a wall of shelves. It held a few books. Frilly hats. A little tea set.

"What's the name of your store again?" I asked, noticing a classic teddy bear on one of the shelves.

She stopped and turned to look at me. "I don't know. I haven't named it yet."

"You haven't—" I watched her closely. She seemed serious.

I'd seen the name over the door. It was something... Gifts or...

"Timeless Keepsakes," I said.

"That's so perfect," she said. "I love it. Timeless Keepsakes it is."

An older woman came into the store. "I need to... um." She gestured toward the woman.

"Go," I said. "I'll wait here."

I wasn't going anywhere. The older woman who just came inside was also wearing a long dress, though it wasn't nearly as fetching on her as it was..."

Hell. I didn't even know the young lady's name.

I was going to stay right here until I figured some things out.

4

ELISE

I was really happy to have customers. It was a good sign that Mrs. Johnson had stopped in. If Mrs. Johnson patronized my store, then others would surely follow.

But while Mrs. Johnson was examining all the glass balls on the Christmas tree, I kept stealing glances with my other, more handsome customer.

He was taller than me. Lean. His hair was short and he was clean-shaven. I'd gotten used to the men around here with their beards, so a clean-shaven man was unusual. And appreciated.

And his eyes smiled when he looked at me.

He propped an elbow on the mantle and watched me.

He made me feel elegant and pretty in the silver dress I had worn just for the occasion of it being the first day of my store opening.

"Can I get some of these pinecones?" Mrs. Johnson asked.

"Of course. How many would you like?"

"I'll take two dozen of the reds and two dozen of the silvers."

"Oh my. Of course." I was going to be spending my evening

dipping more cones in wax. I would make extra. Once the word about Mrs. Johnson buying them got out, then they would go like hotcakes.

"I'll start gathering up those pinecones," I said. "While you look around some more."

I went to the window and picked up the large basket of red pinecones.

I'd gotten no more than a couple of feet carrying the basket in both hands when *he* intercepted me.

"Let me carry that," he said.

"It's not heavy," I said, but he took it out of my hands, anyway and carried it to the counter.

"I'll grab the silver ones," he said.

I went behind the counter, grabbed a box, and started counting out pinecones.

I'd filled the box with a dozen of them, when I looked up to catch of glimpse of the man whose name I did not know. *Him.*

He stood with his back to me, holding the basket of pinecones in both hands. But he was staring outside. Frozen.

I started toward him, took all of two steps to see what he saw, but...

"Can you tell me about these glass balls?" Mrs. Johnson asked, pulling my attention back to her.

"Of course." Mrs. Johnson could be important to my business being successful. And, in truth, I had sunk a substantial amount of my money into it. If it failed... then... I would be at the mercy of my sisters.

Leaving the man to his own devices, I turned and joined Mrs. Johnson at the tree. Explained where I had gotten the glass balls. How each one was unique and handmade.

As Mrs. Johnson studied the different decorations, I looked over shoulder for *him*.

But he wasn't there.

"I'll take this one," she said, putting a glass ball in my hands. "And this one."

I was quite pleased. The glass balls had been a big investment. One of the more risker ones I had made simply because of their delicacy and how far they had to travel to get here. All in all, they had been rather pricey.

But now I had sold three of them in the first day for a handsome profit.

Mrs. Johnson was ready to check out, but I didn't have the silver wax pinecones.

"Excuse me," I said. "I have to get your silver pinecones."

"Take your time, Dear. I'll just take a look at some of these paintings your sister did. So lovely."

I went to the shop window. The basket of pinecones was still sitting there.

Looking around for *him*, I made a complete circle around, but he wasn't here.

I took a deep breath. Maybe he had just stepped outside for some air.

That was completely understandable. But he hadn't brought the basket of pinecones to me.

Thoroughly perplexed, I picked up the basket and carried it to the counter.

My hands shook a little as I counted the two dozen silver pinecones.

There was a good reason he had stepped outside. There had to be.

I was certain of it.

After putting Mrs. Johnson's money in the tin money box my brother-in-law Graham had given me, I smiled and thanked Mrs. Johnson as I handed her the boxes.

I walked with her to the door. Help it open for her as she walked through. Waited a beat. Then stepped out onto the street and looked both ways for *him*.

But the handsome man was not there.

He had vanished.

Oh my.

With a little half smile on my lips, I went back into my shop.

Today was a good day. A very good day.

5

BENJAMIN

I stood on the streets of Whiskey Springs watching as cars and trucks passed on the road.

A police car zipped by, colorful siren blazing.

The place next door, serving up burgers and fries, was hopping with customers. Everybody wanted to get out before the storm blocked them in.

A happy young couple walked in front of me, said hello before they got in line at the burger joint.

I'd always found it interesting how snowfall, especially at Christmas, seemed to bring out the best in people.

The snow was falling. Big fluffy flakes. The pretty snowflakes that came before the deadly deluge of them. The cold air slapped me in the face, bringing me out of what felt like a daze.

I stood just outside a little shop called Timeless Keepsakes. That's what the tasteful little wooden sign hanging on the awning just above the door said, anyway.

I had met a girl.

A girl who had quickened my pulse.

It was a surprise. I had thought my heart had turned

permanently numb after a series of girlfriends gone bad. I couldn't even remember how many of them there had been. Five or six maybe.

The girl—I didn't even know her name—had smiled at me and something had uncoiled in my heart.

But something was not as it should be.

I'd stood inside that shop and looked out the window. I had seen horses and buggies. Wagons. I'd seen people—everyone walking around in historical dress. Women and men. I'd watched enough western movies to know.

I had stood there and I had seen the past.

And now I stood in front of the shop. Looking at the present.

Every so slowly, I forced myself to turn around and face the little shop.

I looked inside the window and saw the very same thing I had seen before I had gone through the door.

A model train chugged on its own little track through a tiny little village.

People moved about inside. People dressed like me looked at books and games and souvenirs.

It was what I was seeing now and what I had seen before.

But it was not what I had seen after I had gone inside.

It had been some kind of trick of the light. Maybe it was some kind of thing they played over the window for ambiance.

But it wasn't there now.

Another possibility... I had imagined it.

I was not that imaginative. I was just a regular guy. Doing regular guy things.

I just needed to go back inside.

Then I could find out whatever kind of trick they had played on me. Playing with my emotions like that.

I took two steps forward. Reached out for the doorknob, but my phone rang.

I could tell by the ringtone that it was my sister. I couldn't keep avoiding her. I had to face this head on and get it over with. She was going to kill me for missing her wedding. But it was not my fault.

Reaching into my pocket for my phone, instead I pulled out a little glass ball wrapped in velvet.

I just stood there in the middle of the sidewalk holding the glass ball.

She had given it to me and I didn't even know her name.

Furthermore, I hadn't paid her. This was something I had to take care of. I was not a thief.

6

ELISE

*I*t was almost time to lock up for the day.

I'd watched as the sunset splashed a rainbow of color over the tall rugged mountains as the sun dropped behind them.

As the day waned, the number of customers had dwindled. But the middle of the day had been very good. It had helped that it was less than one week before Christmas.

My shop, newly dubbed Timeless Keepsakes had everything a person could need to both decorate their home for Christmas and make sure everyone got memorable gifts. Keepsakes.

I locked up and got ready to make the short walk home.

As I had gone through my day, I kept thinking about my very first customer. A handsome man whose name I didn't even know.

It meant something, too, that he was my first customer. I just knew it did. It had to.

It didn't bother me that he had not paid for the glass ball I had given him. Even if it was my favorite. That meant something, too.

I wasn't worried, because I knew he would be back.

I walked home through the twilight, looking forward to the next day.

I understood more than I probably should.

I already knew that he was *the one*.

The man had walked into my shop through the front door and then he had walked back out, vanishing.

Most people would find this troubling.

I found it to be one of the most exciting things possible.

All three of my older sisters had married men from the future. I had watched two of them firsthand and heard about the second one.

I knew how it worked. I knew the story of Vaughn Becquerel. Nearly a century ago, her life had been saved by a spell that had sent her through time.

The spell that ran through her blood had been passed along to her descendants.

Along with the love spell that was part of it.

There was certainly more to the story, but that's what I knew.

It was enough.

It was enough for me to believe that there was a man from the future out there for me.

I was just waiting for him to find me.

My boots crunching on the fallen leaves as I walked toward my house, I replayed my interactions with *him*.

A handsome man, he quickened my heart rate.

And the way he looked at me…

I wondered what his name was.

I also wondered when he would be back.

After waiting for what seemed like forever, he was finally here.

My parents had given birth to five children, evenly spaced out over time, one a year. I was the youngest. Our brother was the middle child.

And for the last four years, my sisters had, one by one, fallen in love with a man from the future.

Our brother had been skipped over. I didn't know what that meant, but I didn't concern myself with it. Colton could take care of himself.

So this was my year. My time.

I had been watching for him.

And now he was here.

He wouldn't know it yet. That was how it worked.

I would have to explain it to him.

Then once he understood, we could be married.

I went inside where Hector, our butler, had supper waiting.

There was one thing though that I wasn't so sure about.

There was no guarantee that he, whoever he was, would choose to stay here in the past.

Just because it had worked out for my sisters, did not guarantee that it would work out so simply for me.

"Good evening, Miss Elise," Hector said. "I have good news for you."

Hector had been our butler since we had come west four years ago. He was a small Chinese man who was loyal as the day was long.

"What's the news?" I asked, stepping into the kitchen.

"Your brother is here," he said. "Colton."

"Where is he?"

"He's upstairs. Would you like to wait for him or do you want to go ahead with supper?"

"I'll wait for him," I said.

I went back into the parlor to wait for my brother to come downstairs.

The grandfather clock chimed six times.

As a shop owner, I was going to have long days.

I loved the idea. I felt like I really had a future with Timeless Keepsakes.

I needed to gather some more pinecones and dip them in wax, but that would have to wait until morning. Tonight I was exhausted.

I would ask Colton to help me gather them.

He was always there when one of us needed him.

7

BENJAMIN

*T*he storm came in hard that night.

Going back to my room, I did some research on the weather. As a pilot, I had become something of a meteorologist myself. Meteorology was a life or death skill for pilots. A little known fact. We could not simply rely on others to predict the weather for us.

I'd known a lot of private pilots who had gotten into trouble by not doing their own due diligence on the weather.

And, if I had to be honest with myself, I could admit that I been a bit lax about this particular trip. I knew that weather in the mountains was more unpredictable than in the south for the most part.

The storm had been unexpected, but now that it was here, it followed predictable winter storm patterns.

And as expected, the town closed down. We had power through the night, but by morning, when the lines got heavy with snow and ice, they began to snap and the power went down.

Fortunately, the bed and breakfast had a fireplace both downstairs in the parlor and one in my bedroom. The downside was that the fireplaces burned real wood. So without power, it took a lot of effort to keep the big house heated.

The staff at the bed and breakfast was prepared. I had to give them that. They had plenty of firewood. Plenty of candles.

Oddly enough, there was only one other guest. The hotels in town were full, but there were only two of us guests at the bed and breakfast. And since that other guest stayed in her room, I hadn't even met her yet.

So I had the run of the place. Undisturbed. The girl behind the desk had gone home last night and wouldn't come back until things cleared up. The cook/housekeeper lived in the house, so he stayed.

He was an older man, about sixty, by the name of Marshall who'd been at the house even before it had become a bed and breakfast ten years ago.

"This is looking like the storm we had back in '18," he said. "Everything was shut down for two weeks."

"Two weeks? They said one week."

"One week of storm. One week to dig out." Marshall said, tossing a clean dish cloth over his shoulder. "Want some coffee?"

"I would love some coffee." We stood in the kitchen, checking the news and weather on our phones. "But how are we going to make coffee without power?"

Marshall grinned. "I have a generator."

I slid my phone into my pocket. "Well, why didn't you say so?"

"It's my first time using it," he said. "And it's a little one. I don't think it'll do much more than run the coffee maker and charge up our phones."

"That's okay," I said. "Can I help you get it going?"

"You know something about generators?" Marshall asked.

"I can figure it out," I said. "I happen to know something about engines."

"Right," Marshall said. "The airplane pilot."

It didn't take long for us to get the generator going along with some coffee.

As we sat together at the kitchen table, a door closed upstairs.

"The other guest?" I asked, knowing it had to be.

"Yeah," Marshall said. "She stays to herself."

"She comes here a lot?" I asked.

Marshall made a face I couldn't read and hid it behind his coffee mug.

"She has a standing room here."

I straightened in my chair. The roar of the generator outside the back door reminded me of sitting in the cockpit of an airplane. Even the heavy orange extension cord didn't bother me.

But for some reason, knowing that there was a woman who had a standing room here at the bed and breakfast sent a shiver down my spine.

"Does she ever come down?" I asked.

"Sometimes," he said. "Rarely. Mostly she calls when she wants me to bring something up for her to eat. I knock and leave it outside the door."

"When does she come out?"

"Don't get me wrong," he said. "When she comes out, she charms everyone. Sometimes goes into town. I think she runs some kind of business. Travels a lot, actually."

I went to the coffee pot, refilled my mug. Added some creamer. It was no latte, but I'd learned how to make do with what I had.

"She comes and goes through the back door," Marshall added. "Uses the back stairs. I rarely even know she's here."

"So basically she lives here," I said.

"Basically."

"How many rooms do you have total not including hers?" I asked.

"Two others."

"So this bed and breakfast is for two rooms?"

"I guess so," Marshall said, going to refill his own coffee. Stir in some sweetener and creamer. "That bothers you?"

"Not really," I said, though for some reason it did. "How did the other places in town know that you had room enough for me?"

Marshall waved it off. "We're the last to fill up. We don't really advertise, you know."

I didn't know. And I had more questions, but decided to leave it alone for now.

"Who did all these paintings?" I asked. "They look original."

"You have a good eye," Marshall said, sitting back down. "They are original. Done by Bailey Auclair. She's well-known around here."

"I saw a lot of her paintings for sell at the Timeless Keepsakes shop in town."

Marshall slowly set his mug on the table.

"Benjamin," he said. "They don't sell Auclair paintings in town anymore."

8

ELISE

"I need to talk to you about something," I said.

The morning sun was warm, but the wind was cold coming off the mountains. Clouds clustered around the mountain peaks. Snowing up there. When the clouds cleared, there would be fresh snow.

That meant it wasn't long before we got a good snowfall here in the valley. It would be the third of the season. The first two had come and gone, melting the next day.

"What is it?" Colton added three pinecones to the basket. "How many of these do you need?"

"They're selling really well. I can't have too many. I need to tell you something."

Colton straightened and looked at me. "What's wrong?" he asked.

"Nothing," I said. "Everything is wonderful."

Colton narrowed his eyes.

A couple of chipmunks scurried around us, giving us dirty looks for taking their pinecones.

"So what is it that you need to talk to me about?" Colton asked.

I set my basket down and clasped my hands together in front of me.

"I think he's here," I said, my voice unnecessarily low. We were the only ones out here, at least a mile away from civilization.

It was a bit of a walk, but this area had the best pine tree cones. Except for a few, they managed to fall perfectly without damaging themselves as they hit the ground. I took it as a sign.

Colton reached down, swept up a couple more pinecones. Tossed them into the basket. "Who's here?"

I smiled. With four sisters, nothing much fazed him.

"The man I'm going to marry."

Now he stood perfectly still, a pinecone in each hand. The wind whipped at his cloak, but he seemed unconcerned by the cold.

"I didn't realize you were being courted by anyone."

And I wasn't easily fazed either. "I'm not."

"When did you start looking for a husband?" Colton was looking at me sideways now. "Have you signed up for one of those mail order bride things?"

"What? No. I'm not looking for a husband."

"You just said—"

The wind whipped at the hood of my cloak and I grabbed hold of it, pulling it close. "I said he's here."

"Okay," Colton said. "So you found a man you like." He gazed up at the sky, studying the clouds. "We need to get back. I think it's going to snow."

I crossed my arms. "Colton," I said. "I think he's from the future."

Colton froze.

"Why would you think that?"

"Because he looked... different... and he was there one minute and then walked outside my shop and vanished."

"What does that have to do with you finding the man you're going to marry?"

"Well since Andrea, Bailey, and Dakota all married men from the future, it makes sense that I would be next."

Colton silently picked up the basket of pinecones and we started down the trail that led toward the grove of aspen trees.

"Elise," he said. "Just because a man comes from the future doesn't mean he wants to stay here, much less get married to you."

"Never mind," I said. "I'm not going to talk to you about this. You don't understand."

"I just think you're putting your cart before your horses."

I had no response for that.

Men. Men just did not understand.

He would see. When the man came back, Colton would understand.

BENJAMIN

I stayed inside for most of the day.

Now and then I heard footsteps walking around in the other guest room.

After prowling the house for what seemed like hours, I decided it was time to take a walk downtown.

I had bought myself some good snow boots, so it didn't matter to me that it was still snowing. I actually liked it that no one else would be out and about.

I wanted to look around on my own some without anyone else distracting me.

After bundling up, I slipped outside without telling anyone. As far as I was concerned, no one needed to know where I was.

I had gotten no more than a few feet when I started to second-guess myself. The conditions were near white-out.

But I was committed now.

It wasn't hard to find my way downtown, even in the blinding snow. It was a little eerie that there were no cars on the road, but I figured that was actually a good thing. People were listening to the authorities. Staying home and staying safe. *Hunker down*, they advised. Stay warm.

I knew where I was headed. I was headed to Timeless Keepsakes.

I had not been able to get the girl out of my mind.

Of course, I knew that she wouldn't be there today. The town was closed down. All I wanted to do was to peek inside the window.

As I neared the shop, a police car, sporting big snow tires, slowly made its way along the snow-covered street. I kept my head down. I wasn't doing anything wrong, but I didn't need the police getting the wrong idea.

As the police slowly drove past, I kept walking on past Timeless Keepsakes. Just a man out taking a stroll in the snowstorm.

With the police turning down another street, out of sight now, I turned around and started back.

My heart started racing as I reached the little shop.

Timeless Keepsakes.

I was wondering about my own sanity right about now.

I was out in a snowstorm stalking, not so much a girl, but a shop I had seen. A shop that should not have been.

Marshall's words replayed in my head. *They don't sell Auclair paintings in town.*

I hadn't gotten a chance to ask why.

It didn't matter why so much as it mattered that I had seen them. For sale. In the shop.

Maybe Marshall didn't know. It was a fleeting thought, but I dismissed it as quickly as it formed. Marshall had been certain.

And I believed him.

I passed the door to the shop. Then stepped up to the window.

Everything was dark inside. The little train sat idle on the tracks. The model village was locked down, too, in the midst of its own faux snow storm.

I didn't see anything out of the ordinary. I pressed my forehead against the cold glass, a hand over my eyes.

I couldn't see much from here, but I didn't see any paintings on the walls. And instead of the open area that I had been in yesterday, there were rows of display shelves.

This was definitely not the place had been yesterday.

I turned and looked up and down the deserted street.

There was no one out. Certainly no horses and buggies. No people dressed in period dress.

Period dress.

A flash to the past.

Turning back around, I stared at the doorknob.

No. I should not.

ELISE

I spent several hours making more wax dipped pinecones. Red and Silver. I contemplated adding green ones to my inventory and made a mental note to stop by the General Store to check for green dye.

I had a lot of customers, over a dozen throughout the day. Considering how small Whiskey Springs was, I considered that to be a lot.

When I wasn't busy with customers, I stood at the window, pinecones baskets refilled, and watched the street.

I regretted talking to Colton about *him.*

Colton was too grounded in what he considered reality.

He knew that my sisters married men from the future, but he was too logical to entertain the notion that I might also find a man from the future.

That just showed how much more time I had spent thinking about this.

Too much, truth be told. But when three of your sisters marry men from the future, it bears thinking about.

I hadn't talked to any of my sisters about this, not really. I had figured this out all on my own.

Apparently, when I'd picked Colton to talk to, I'd picked the wrong sibling.

But he was the only one available.

Andrea lived in Denver. Bailey and Dakota lived on the other side of the mountain. On top of the mountain, actually.

The clock on the mantle chimed the hour. Six o'clock. Time for me to close down my shop and go home.

And disappointment settled over me like a veil. The handsome man had not come back today. I had been so looking forward to seeing him again. Finding out everything about him. Including his name.

Maybe Colton was right. Maybe I was putting my cart before my horses.

Going back behind the counter, I grabbed a piece of peppermint. I put on my cloak, then picked up my reticule and looped it over my wrist.

After blowing out the lantern on the counter, I turned, ready to go now.

I froze.

The man was standing there in the middle of my shop. The little bell over the door had not rung this time.

He looked a bit dazed and confused, but when he saw me, his face lit up.

"Hi," he said.

I swallowed.

I'd been watching for him all day, but now that he was here, I could hardly believe it.

"You came back," I said, a slow smile spreading across my lips.

He smiled, too.

"How could I not?" he asked, closing the distance between us, but not touching me.

"Are you the one?" I asked.

Confusion again.

"The one?"

"The man from the future?" I asked. "For me?"

"Yes," he said.

I wanted to touch him. Lifted my hands to put on his arms, but stopped myself. My smile faltered

Something was wrong.

I gazed into his sapphire blue eyes, searching for answers.

It occurred to me then. He wasn't supposed to know.

None of the men who came to the past knew that they were going to marry my sisters. Not at first.

I knew, but only because of them.

But he wasn't supposed to know.

11

BENJAMIN

I felt compelled to touch her. To simply connect with her. This beautiful girl I had not been able to stop thinking about. But, although she smiled at me, she seemed hesitant.

Her eyes were siren green. The kind of eyes a man couldn't look away from even if he wanted to. I didn't want to.

I was in the same version of the shop I had been in yesterday when I had first seen her.

It had the same fresh-smelling fir tree decorated in red and silver pinecones, ribbons, and glass balls.

The girl was the same, except that her dress was different. Yesterday she had been wearing a long silver dress. Today she wore a pretty magenta dress with a black cloak over it.

And her hair was pulled back and secured over one shoulder.

She remembered me. Almost seemed to expect me. Except... when I agreed that I was *the one*, she retreated a bit. I didn't even know what she meant by *the one*. And I certainly didn't know what she meant about me being from the future.

I only knew that I was enchanted with her.

I was drawn to her.

"What is your name?" I asked, not wanting to go another minute without having a name to put to her.

"Elise," she said.

Elise. That name sounded familiar.

"I'm Benjamin."

She smiled again. "Benjamin," she said. "That's a good name."

"I think so." A wagon rumbled past outside. "Can you explain to me what's happening?" I asked.

"I—" She shook her head. "I don't think so. Not yet."

"Why not?" I asked with a little smile.

She turned around, her skirts rustling, and took a step away. But she glanced back over her shoulder.

"It's too soon," she said.

"So is there some kind of timeline?"

"Not really," she said.

I turned and walked to the window. Leaned forward so I could see better.

There was no snow. Only a clear, sunny day.

Instead of a deserted snow-covered road, I saw men on horseback. Horses and buggies. People in period dress walking.

Just like yesterday.

Wherever I had gone yesterday, I had come back here today.

"What do you see?" Elise asked.

"I see a beautiful young lady," I said, turning to face her.

"Outside?"

"Right in front of me."

She smiled.

"You're on your way out," I said, noticing her handbag and cloak.

"Yes," she said, a little frown creasing her brow.

I didn't want to leave her.

"Can you stay a moment?" I asked. "We never finished my tour."

"Your tour?" She tucked a strand of hair behind an ear.

I nodded toward the shelf behind her, pulled off my leather gloves and stuck them in my pockets.

"Okay," she said. "Where were we?"

As I walked toward the shelf, I noticed a painting with a herd of bighorn sheep on a mountainside. Most significant about the painting was that the sky was lavender blue.

I leaned close enough to read the signature. Auclair. October 20, 1868. "Are these paintings for sale?" I asked.

"Of course," she said. "Everything is."

"Tell me about that bear," I said before she could say more. I had questions but I wanted to think things through first. To know what it was I was asking.

I noticed her hands trembled a bit as she took the teddy bear from the shelf.

"This bear was made by a woman right here in Whiskey Springs."

"You're kidding me," I said, taking the bear from her and examining it closely in the dim light. The seams were small and perfect. I was no expert, but I never would have guessed it to be handmade.

"No," she said. "Her name is Savannah and she makes them for her children."

"I'm surprised this hasn't sold," I said, handing the bear back to her.

As she took the bear, her fingers brushed against mine.

I felt a jolt. I honestly felt a jolt shoot through my system.

She looked up at me, her eyes wide, and neither one of us moved.

We stood there, the teddy bear between us, our fingers touching ever so lightly.

The blood raced through my veins. I had never had such a reaction to simply brushing a woman's fingers.

I set the bear back on the shelf, then cupped her elbows.

"It's a pleasure to meet you Elise," I said.

"And you," she said, her lips were slightly parted, her eyes wide.

I was quite simply a man lost.

Without even thinking, I dipped my head and kissed her on the lips.

Her lips were sweet and so soft and...

I was in a world of trouble.

"Can I walk you home?" I asked.

She smiled up at me.

Trouble.

12

ELISE

The evening sun splashed a lovely ray of color across the mountain peaks as the sun dropped for the evening.

Piano music drifted from the saloon three doors down.

The town changed at night. It didn't become rowdy, necessarily, but ladies were inside their homes. The only ones out and about, for the most part, were men. And, well, it was a saloon, after all.

As a shop owner, I was out later than most ladies, but I was typically home no later than a few minutes past six o'clock.

Tonight was different. Tonight I was out later than usual. I would be walking home in the dark.

But he was here. Benjamin.

I felt like I was walking on clouds.

And then he kissed me.

As his lips touched mine, I knew my life would never be the same again.

I wasn't sure exactly how it was going to change, but I knew it was going to be different.

As we reached the door, I stopped to blow out the candles on either side the door.

It was dark now, darker inside the store than outside.

Benjamin opened the door and held it while I walked through.

I stepped onto the sidewalk and reached into my reticule for my key.

Mr. Johnson, the man who ran the General Store walked past and greeted me.

"Don't forget to lock up," he said. "Looks to be a rowdy evening."

I held up my key. "I won't," I said. "Have a good night, Mr. Johnson."

He tipped his hat and went on his way. I turned around, a smile on my face.

But... Benjamin was not there.

I stepped back inside my shop, but he was not there either.

"Benjamin?" I called out.

No answer.

I even walked through the dark to the room in the back.

But there was enough early evening moonlight coming through window to tell me that he wasn't there either.

I walked back to the door. Stepped outside and locked up.

He had quite simply vanished.

My heart sank.

It wasn't supposed to work like this. Was it?

Walking home in the soft moonlight, I searched my memory for how things had gone with my sisters when they first met their husbands. All of their men had stayed for longer than a minute.

I was at a loss.

None of my sisters were here to talk to. And I could not talk to Colton about it. He had made that clear this morning.

I could still feel Benjamin's lips against mine. My first kiss.

I'd waited a lifetime for this moment.

He was the one. I knew it just as sure as I knew anything.

But how was I supposed to be with him if he wasn't here?

I sat down at my desk and began to write a letter.

DEAR BENJAMIN,

I know you had to go. That you had no choice.

I'll just say it. Please come back.

If you believe... If you believe in us...

Meet me at the park at Twilight tonight. Christmas Eve.

I'll be there. Waiting for you.

No matter when. I'll be there.

Please don't leave me here without you.

Yours forever,

Elise

13

BENJAMIN

$\mathcal{I}$ stood on the sidewalk in front of the snow-covered street.

The wind, howling around the buildings, blew snow into my face, stinging sharply.

I could still taste the peppermint from Elise's lips. I could still feel her lips on mine.

But I had walked through the door and been dumped onto the street.

It took me a minute to realize what had happened. That Elise was no longer in front of me. By the time I figured it out, the door to the shop was closed.

I turned the knob, trying to open the door again, but it was locked.

Then I saw the police car slowly making its way back along the street.

I turned, as smoothly as possible, and walked along the sidewalk the way I had come. Toward the bed and breakfast.

My heart was pounding far too fast. Part of it was probably the danger of being arrested for breaking and entering by the bored police officer. But most of it was from kissing Elise.

I should not have kissed her.

A reasonable man would not have kissed her.

She was a stranger to me. A girl I just met. And not just any girl.

I looked over my shoulder at the deserted streets. Watched the police car turn down another side road.

A girl who wasn't supposed to be.

Before going inside the bed and breakfast, I took a walk around the to the back. The generator was off so everything was quiet. Just my footsteps in the snow and the howling of the wind around the building.

I stopped at the back of the house and looked up toward the second-floor windows.

Marshall said there was a woman who practically lived in one of the rooms upstairs, only coming down on occasion.

She comes and goes through the back door. Uses the back stairs.

I couldn't think of any reason for Marshall to lie to me. What purpose would it serve? After a few days, perhaps a week or two at the very most, I would be gone from here and he would never see me again.

What did I care if a woman used one of the rooms upstairs?

Sure. I had asked about others. Since we were stranded here together, I kind of needed to know who I was stranded with.

Other than that, I had no reason to know or care.

A flock of chickadees landed on the ground, then seeming to notice me standing there, took flight.

There was a back door, but there were no back stairs.

I glanced up toward the second floor, but had no reason to stay out here. Retracing my steps, I went back around to the front door and went inside the house.

Unwrapping from my coat, scarf, and gloves I started upstairs.

The grandfather clock chimed the hour. Seven o'clock.

Back in my room, I lit a few candles and paced my room.

I didn't want to go downstairs right now, but I felt edgy. Unsettled.

It was on one of those paces across the room that I stopped and studied the painting on the wall beside the door.

Grabbing a candle, I held it close.

It was the same. Bighorn sheep on the side of a mountain. A lavender blue sky.

The signature was the same.

Auclair.

October 20, 1868.

14

ELISE

I woke early the next morning. I had hardly slept the night before.

I kept replaying the events of the past couple of days over and over in my head.

I'd met Benjamin. He'd vanished.

Then he had reappeared.

And he had kissed me.

Any doubt I had that he was the one for me from the future was erased.

Even if he wasn't from the future, I did not care.

I'd tossed and turned. Trying to sort it out.

Maybe he wasn't from the future.

I'd had no indication that he was one way or the other.

It didn't matter to me.

I was charmed by him.

Was this how my sisters had felt when they had met their husbands to be? Had they just known?

Snow clouds filled the sky. It was going to snow.

Everyone liked snow at Christmastime. It would make it

harder for people to get to my shop, but that was okay. I would take a white Christmas any day.

Besides, it wasn't customers that I was interested in so much right now.

It was a certain charming, clean-shaven man who wore a black wool coat.

One who stood right there and kissed me in my shop.

I hummed to myself as I brushed out my hair. One hundred strokes just as my mother had taught us.

I refused to think about the possibility that I might never see him again.

For me that wasn't an option. I was going to see him again.

He was the one I was going to marry.

I dressed quickly and went downstairs.

It was definitely colder today.

"Good morning," Hector said. "Would you like some hot tea?"

"You read my mind, Hector," I said, sliding into one of the kitchen chairs. "What would I do without you?"

"You'd probably go off to live with one of your sisters," he said.

I nodded. "You're actually probably right."

"How's the shop coming along?"

"It's going really well," I said, then I leaned my elbows on the table while I waited for Hector to heat the water for my tea.

"You were here when Andrea met Reed, right?" I asked, dipping my toe into a conversation that I had never had with Hector.

"That's right," he said, showing no reaction.

"And Bailey and Graham."

"Yes ma'am."

He handed me a steaming cup of tea.

"Did you notice anything odd?"

"I try not to notice things, especially things that are odd," Hector said.

I just laughed and sipped my tea. "You should be a politician, Hector," I said.

"And then who would take care of you?" he asked.

"Good point." The warm mug warmed my hands and the steam felt good to my skin. "Hector?"

"Yes ma'am?"

"Never mind," I said.

I couldn't talk to Hector about my fanciful ideas. The thing with Benjamin was just something I had to figure out for myself.

And I would.

I would figure it out.

And when I saw Benjamin again, we would figure it out together.

"The weather looks bad," I said. "Would you mind packing some food in case I get stuck at the shop?"

"Of course," he said. "Do you want me to go with you?"

Maybe. Except for Benjamin.

"No. You stay here and hold down the fort. I'm probably just being overly worrisome."

But an idea was forming in the back of my mind.

15

BENJAMIN

*T*he storm picked up again during the night, leaving a mess outside. Snow covered sidewalks. Limbs down. Even a few trees.

Fortunately, Marshall and I got the generator going and were able to keep our phones charged.

I had a particularly unpleasant conversation with my sister. Apparently, she had turned into Bridezilla.

"Unfortunate timing," Marshall said as I hung up. I'd already told him that I was going to be missing my sister's wedding in four days. Christmas Eve.

"For her, anyway," I said.

It wasn't my fault she was getting married on Christmas Eve and it wasn't my fault I was snowed in and couldn't get out.

If it had been me in her shoes, I liked to think I would have been more worried about my little brother's safety than him missing my wedding. But I could understand her point of view. She'd been planning this wedding for two years. Frankly, I would more than happy to see it in the rearview window.

A door slammed upstairs.

"Has she been down today?" I asked.

"Nah," Marshall said. "I took a tray of food up to her at lunch.

"What does she do all day?"

Marshall shrugged. Kept his face blank. "Work," he said vaguely.

"The door?" I asked. "Where is she going?"

"Out the back," he said.

I didn't bother to point out that with this storm, there was nowhere for her to go. Out back or otherwise.

I took a piece of cheese and a cracker from the cheese tray Marshall had made. "Don't have to go to all this trouble just for me," I said.

"I don't mind," he said. "Besides, I'd rather we ate the cheese than have it spoil and have to throw it out."

I also decided not to point out that I had looked and there were no back stairs.

"What kind of work?" I asked.

"Sorry?" Marshall put the crackers away and the cheese cutter in the sink.

"What kind of work did you say she does?"

"Oh," Marshall said. "I don't ask her much. She's very private."

I nodded and bit into a cracker. But I wasn't buying it. The woman practically lived here and Marshall was claiming he didn't even know what kind of work she did that kept her cooped up in her room.

"She has a suite," he said. "A bedroom, sitting room, and a little office."

"Good to know," I said.

"I'm sure you'll meet her," Marshall said, taking out a broom and going to work on the floor.

I wasn't so sure. I'd been here a few days now and I hadn't so much as seen her. Just a slamming door now and then. Not really slamming. Just closing. But in the big, empty house, it sounded like slamming, especially when the generator was off.

The clock chimed the hour. It was eleven o'clock.

"The weather looks rough out there," Marshall said. "You going to try to go for a walk? They're saying it's best to stay inside."

"I don't know," I said. I wanted to, but the weather was looking too bad today for even me to go out.

Besides, I'd had a lot to think about.

Not that I had gotten anywhere with that thinking.

"What did you say the woman's name was?" I asked.

There was something about the mystery woman upstairs that I wasn't able to let go of.

"Not sure I said." Marshall emptied the dust pan in the trashcan. "But her name is Vaughn."

16

ELISE

I took the basket Hector had packed for me and set it in the back room that served as my office, my storage room, and my work room.

A large wooden table in the middle of the room was littered with pinecones, dried wax, and jars of red and silver dye. Mr. Johnson at the General Store didn't have any green dye and the silver dye had come from Graham, my sister's husband.

He never said where he got it, so I didn't know where to get more. I had written my sister a letter, but I hadn't gotten a response yet. The mail was erratic these days, at best.

At any rate, I would soon have only red wax pinecones to sell.

It was odd that I was selling more wax coated pinecones than anything else. A novelty, I suppose.

I had actually sold a couple of my sister's paintings. One of a Christmas tree and a fireplace. I knew it was based on her own house. The other one of a cabin in the woods. I didn't know what that was based off of. Maybe just her imagination.

I felt better now that I had a plan. When, not if, but when Benjamin came back I knew what to do.

During my sleepless night, I had figured it out.

It was the door. The door to my shop.

Benjamin had come through the door both times and I was pretty sure he had vanished back out through that same door.

So the door was the portal.

When he came back, we would just stay in my shop. I didn't know what we'd do from there, but I was pretty sure we could figure it out.

I opened the front door and with it being just days from Christmas, I had customers all morning.

My little metal money box was filling up nicely.

It was after lunch before I had time to so much as grab a biscuit. If I was going to stay this busy all the time, then I would have to look into hiring someone to help me out.

Walking around as I ate, I ended up at the window. I closed my eyes and wished really hard for Benjamin to come back. I wanted to see him more than anything.

I wanted to kiss him again. I had replayed that kiss a million times.

Then I got busy again and only had time for quick glances toward the door.

Benjamin did not come back.

A young Irish gentleman named Eamon Hastings came by and asked for help picking out of gift for his mother. He was young, about my age, and seemed a little nervous.

I helped him choose a glass ornament with an elk inside it. I wrapped it up in paper, since I had run out of velvets cloths a while back.

I smiled as I handed it to him.

"Miss Elise," he said, keeping his eyes down and taking the wrapped ornament from me. "I was wondering if I might call on you."

"Excuse me?" My smile almost faltered, but I was a businesswoman. So I kept the smile on my lips.

"My family just moved here and I don't know anyone. My Ma says you're not married. Do you think I might call on you sometime?"

"Of course," I said. "Sometime. If you'll excuse me, I have to see what Mrs. Johnson needs."

I slipped around him, as calmly and smoothly as I could manage, considering that my instinct was to flee. As I moved past him, I detected an odd smell. Something like a wet goat.

I covered my mouth for a second, but shook it off as I approached Mrs. Johnson standing next to the Christmas tree.

"How can I help you, Mrs. Johnson?"

"I just need a couple more of those pinecones," she said. "In silver."

"You're in luck," I said. "I only have three left."

"I'll take all three then," she said. Then she leaned closer and lowered her voice. "That young man, Eamon, lives just down the road from me and my husband. He comes from a good family. I haven't met them, but I know they're good people."

"Oh," I said, carefully wrapping her pinecones to go, wondering how she knew anything about Eamon's family when she hadn't met them.

"He's a good catch," she said. "Good husband material. He's working as an assistant to Dr. Avery."

I suppose I was supposed to be impressed by Eamon. That he came from a good family. That was working as an assistant to Dr. Avery.

I put her pinecones in a bag and handed it to her. "Thank you," I said. "But I'm not looking for a husband."

"A woman alone like you," she said. "Living along. Running a shop. Needs a husband. Else people might get the wrong idea."

"My brother lives with me."

"Just trying to be helpful," Mrs. Johnson said. "Since I know you don't have your parents to watch after you."

"I appreciate your concern," I said.

"You know how people are," she said. "A woman living alone. They start to think of her as a woman of ill-repute."

I forced myself to close my dropping draw.

"Well, give it some thought, my dear," she said. "Merry Christmas."

"Merry Christmas," I said, watching her leave.

It was four days until Christmas.

The shop was suddenly empty.

I hurried to the door and locked it. Enough customers for one day.

Going to the back room, I busied my hands with straightening things up.

I told myself Mrs. Johnson was only trying to be helpful. But her words stung.

They stung on several different fronts.

She was right about my parents. My father had been killed in the war. Then my mother had passed away not too long after that.

Our uncle gambled away our house, but my oldest sister Andrea had gotten to our money in the bank before Uncle had.

Then the five of us had come west.

At the time we had not known that our father had bought a house for us—the house I was living in right now.

My three older sisters had married well. The oldest had taken her share of the money, but the other two had passed their shares along to me.

Granted, I had put a substantial amount of my money into this shop, but it was going well.

After straightening my supplies, I wiped off the table. Then I found a broom and swept all the little bits of pinecones and wax and dirt tracked from outside into a dustpan.

I wasn't looking for a husband. I didn't *need* a husband. Wanting and needing were too different things, after all.

I might *want* to marry Benjamin, but I didn't *need* to marry anyone.

Eamon did not interest me in the least.

But now Mrs. Johnson had me thinking about my reputation. It had never occurred to me that being a single woman might hurt my business.

I emptied the dustpan into the wastebasket.

I had a feeling Mrs. Johnson had no idea how much work running a shop was. Just because her husband ran the General Store didn't mean she knew. I was quite proud of everything I had done and I had done it by myself.

I was a little bit offended that she thought I had to have a husband to be successful. That was what I took from her words. She had been suggesting that without a husband, people would come to see me as a woman of ill-repute. She had actually said those words.

Well. As I put away my broom, my gaze landed on the basket of food Hector had packed for me. Looked like I wasn't going to need it today, so I'd just leave it here until I did.

I wandered back into my shop.

Let them think whatever they wanted to think.

I stood in front of the window and watched as a late evening carriage lumbered into town and the driver tossed people's trunks to the ground. Two men and a woman stepped out of the carriage.

This town was growing. They needed a shop like mine. And no matter what Mrs. Johnson said, I wasn't going to marry someone just for the sake of being married.

17

BENJAMIN

*B*y evening I was exhausted. Not from doing anything. On the contrary. It was from doing nothing.

I'd had phone conversations with my sister and my mother. That was exhausting enough.

I'd finally settled in front of the parlor fireplace with a glass of wine and book.

I'd contemplated taking a walk down to Timeless Keepsakes, several times throughout the day.

Not only did I want to solve the mystery of what I was seeing, but I also just plain wanted to see Elise again.

I kept replaying that kiss over and over. I should not have kissed her, but telling myself that did nothing to stop me from wanting to do it again.

I laid my book down and tossed a couple of logs on the fire. I took the poker and rearranged the logs, sending sparks up the chimney to land wherever they might land on the winter wonderland outside.

Marshall was baking something. A pie, maybe. I'd decided that he liked to stay busy, too.

I returned the poker, then straightened and turned.

A movement caught my attention.

A woman was walking down the stairs.

She was a slim, attractive woman wearing blue jeans and a sweatshirt. She had on lace up boots that seemed more for looks than hiking.

She saw me and smiled.

Older than me, I thought. Maybe thirty something.

"Good evening," she said, coming my way.

"You must be Vaughn," I said. "I was beginning to think you didn't really exist."

"I get that a lot," she said. "Do you mind if I join you?"

"Please," I said. "Can I get you a glass of wine?"

"That would be lovely," she said, sitting gracefully on the armchair nearest the fire.

"I'll be right back," I said.

I didn't see Marshall in the kitchen, so I just grabbed a glass and the bottle of wine.

I filled her glass and refilled my own. As a private pilot I was accustomed to serving others. People often didn't realize that private pilots were often not only the pilot, but also the server.

"Thank you," she said. "I apologize for not coming down sooner, but I had some things I needed to take care of."

"No need to apologize," I said. "If I had something to do, I would be doing it. I'm going a bit stir crazy myself."

"The storm will pass in due time," she said, then held up her glass. "To time."

"To time," I said, trying to ignore the tingling at the back of my neck.

"So what have you been doing?" she asked.

"Just reading," I said.

Vaughn had a serenity about her. A classic beauty. Now that I was close enough to look into her green eyes, I couldn't tell how old she was. One of those women who didn't age, I decided.

"Marshall said you have an office up there," I said. "What kind of work do you do?"

"I'm something of a storyteller," she said.

"Oh? What are you working on?"

She settled back in her chair, made herself comfortable.

"A fanciful tale," she said. "Would you like me to tell you a story?"

"Sure," I said, sitting back myself. The book I was reading hadn't caught my attention anyway.

She smiled in such a way that made me think of Elise.

Not surprising. Everything made me think of Elise.

"The story begins in the late 1700s. There was a young girl who lived with her parents in France. Living in the country, the little girl spent her days happily chasing butterflies and dreams."

I smiled.

"Then one day, very unexpectedly, her parents were killed. Tragically. Having no other family, the little girl was sent to live with in a convent with nuns."

"Nuns? That must have been quite a change."

"It was. The girl... we'll call her Miss Dupre... was devastated. But the nuns loved her and they raised her to be good person."

She took a breath. Sipped her wine. Then continued.

"This was during the time America was being settled. Men were looking for wives, but good, moral ladies were hard to find. The only women available were mostly prostitutes and other women of ill-repute. So the governors of the colonies put out a call for good women to come to America. To marry the men. They called them casket girls because they came over here with nothing but a bag they called a casket.

Vaughn had a faraway look in her eyes.

"Is this a true story?" I asked.

"That really happened," she said. "I did my research."

I smiled to encourage her to go on, curious where she was going with this.

"So anyway, Miss Dupre was of an age to be married. She would have stayed with the nuns, but they believed that she should have a family. Not really a nun at heart. They made her a wedding dress and put her on a boat to America. She was to marry a man in Natchez, Mississippi. She had never met him, of course.

"The trip across the sea was hard. A lot of good people didn't make it. Miss Dupre made a friend. A girl her age named Mary. They survived the voyage without incident and traveled up the Mississippi River. They hadn't been on land for very long when they were attacked by Indians."

The fire crackled in the fireplace. The only sound in the house. The generator was off and the snow outside fell silently.

"There was a terrible thunderstorm. Miss Dupree was the only one who survived."

"How?" I asked. I held my wine glass, all but forgotten.

"There was an old man. A Druid." She shook her head. "I don't know where he came from, but he asked her if she wanted to live. She did, of course."

Vaughn turned and looked at me with green eyes so deep, for just a moment, I thought they flashed.

"How did he do it?" I asked.

"He cast a spell. A spell that made a rip in time and sent her through it. To the future."

I held my breath. She was telling me this for a reason.

"The rip in time never healed."

Staring into the fire, I couldn't think about anything other than Elise.

I'm not sure how long we sat there in silence. Finally, I realized that she had stopped talking and looked back at her.

"What happened next?" I asked.

"That's enough for now," she said.

18

ELISE

*S*omeone in the saloon was playing Christmas music on the piano.

Outside, snow came down like silent rain.

I'd known it was going to snow. And it was beautiful.

People complained, of course. People complained about everything. Even if there was nothing they could do about it. They just liked to complain.

I stood in my little shop, getting ready to open for the day.

Christmas Eve was day after tomorrow. Three days until Christmas.

This had always been my favorite time of year. This year, though, it was more of a struggle. It was the second Christmas in a row that I had spent it apart from my sisters.

Colton was here in town. Somewhere. As far as I knew. I actually had not seen him lately.

I had decided to ignore Mrs. Johnson. I put her in the category of complainers. Jealous maybe. A lot of ladies were afraid that single women would steal their husbands away. It was just the silliest thing. I didn't even remember who had told me that. I think it was my sister Bailey. Bailey was wise to the way of the world.

I had lain awake last night trying to imagine what Bailey would say about Mrs. Johnson and her preposterous notion that as a businesswoman I needed a husband.

I finally decided that Bailey would simply laugh it off and tell me that Mrs. Johnson was simply jealous.

So that was what I was going with.

I rearranged my shop window. I removed the baskets of pinecones and sat the teddy bear squarely in the center, propping him up, a little stack of books behind him.

There. The little fellow needed a home for Christmas and this should do it.

The clock chimed nine times.

I unlocked the door and went behind the counter to wait.

When no one walked in, I picked up a book and started to read.

It was over an hour later when I realized that not a single person had come inside my shop.

It was the snow, I decided. The snow was keeping people home.

I went to the window and looked out.

It wasn't the snow.

People continued to go about their daily business. Walking around in the snow like it wasn't even there.

I grabbed a piece of peppermint and wandered around my shop.

With Christmas Eve being day after tomorrow, perhaps everyone had what they needed.

I would just be patient. Every business, especially a new one like this, had slow times.

After checking the door, making sure it was unlocked, I went into the back and sat down to tie some cloth bows to place here and there.

I had half a dozen bows tied when the bell over the door tinkled.

Finally. I had a customer.

Taking the bows with me, I went out into the shop.

I laid them on the counter and looked around for my customer.

Then I saw him.

My heart lodged in my throat.

It was Benjamin.

He was standing in front of the window, his back to me, looking out.

He turned when I came up to stand next to him.

"I don't know how this has happened," he said, looking quite perplexed. "But I think I've gone back in time."

Biting my lip, I smiled. "It's a thing," I said.

"So it seems," he said. "Can you help me understand?"

"I can try," I said. "Just... Just don't go through that door."

19

BENJAMIN

"So that's it?" I asked. "It's just that simple?"

"And that hard." Elise sat back and smiled with a little shrug.

Two hours after coming into Timeless Keepsakes, I had another facet of the story Vaughn had told me.

Elise had three older sisters, all of whom had married men from the future.

"Have you ever heard of a lady named Vaughn?" I asked.

Elise shook her head. "I don't think so."

"I think she has something to do with this time travel thing."

"Well, it had to start somewhere," she said. "Somehow."

"You believe it then?" I asked.

She gave me a look. "You're here aren't you?"

"You say here is 1869."

"I'd take you outside. Show you around, but I believe the door is your portal."

"Don't you think it's odd that everyone has a different portal?"

"Don't you think it's odd that there are portals at all?" she asked.

I laughed. "Yes. It is odd."

"Are you hungry?" she asked, pulling a basket toward her. "Hector sent food in case I got snowed in or…" she shrugged. "Something."

I watched her as she put biscuits on two plates. "Something meaning me?" I asked.

She handed me a plate. "Yes," she admitted with a little smile. "You."

"How did you know it was me?"

"Do you think it's you?"

I leaned forward and, gently placing my hands on her cheeks, I kissed her lightly on the lips.

"Yes," I said. "I think it's you."

She smiled. "Me too."

"There's one problem, though," I said.

"There are probably a lot of problems."

"No, really," I said. "Am I supposed to just live here in your shop?"

She bit her lip again. Somehow this didn't seem to have occurred to her.

"It's a nice shop," she said.

"It is a nice shop," I said, "But I think there has to be a better way."

"I have no doubt about that," she said, taking a bite of her biscuit. "We just have to figure it out."

"How can you be so sure that we can figure this out?"

"I've seen it happen before," she said. "It always seems impossible at first."

"Okay," I said. "Let's see what happens."

"Really?" She seemed surprised.

"Why not?" I asked. "But here's the thing. If I can't leave, then you can't leave."

"Well… how are we going to survive?"

"I don't know," I said.

She shook her head. "I don't know if that will work."

"Maybe the time travel has some kind of time mechanism on it."

"Like what?"

"Maybe we have to stay together for a certain amount of time. You said that the men stayed for a while with your sisters."

"Yes, before they figured it out."

"We already have it figured out," I said. "So maybe we're just ahead of the game."

"Maybe," she said, but she did not seem convinced.

We sat in silence for a few minutes.

"Why don't you have any customers?" I asked.

"Because Mrs. Johnson called me a woman of ill-repute."

"A what?" I said, trying not to laugh at the preposterous statement.

"She said it's because I'm a business owner. And single." She gathered up our empty plates. Then she clasped her hands together in front of her.

The snow had turned to ice, little stinging pellets slamming against the window.

The storm here, in this time, was getting bad. Worse, perhaps, even than it was in the future.

Yet in a lot of ways, the storms now and in the future were mirroring each other.

I wondered how often that happened.

Was it a sign?

Did it mean that things were aligning?

There was so much I did not understand.

Vaughn had told me a story about a young girl from France whose life had been saved by escaping through a rip in time.

The rip never healed.

Somehow the story of Miss Dupre was related to what was happening to me. I just didn't know how yet.

I needed to get back to the bed and breakfast. To ask Vaughn to explain. Maybe she understood why I seemed to be in the past.

But Elise didn't want me to walk through that door.

She believed the door was the portal. If I walked through that door, I would go back to my time. To the future.

And I was inclined to believe her.

So I could either stay here with Elise or I could walk through that door to possibly find an explanation for how I was here.

Insanity.

The whole dilemma was absolutely insane.

20

ELISE

*B*enjamin was right, of course. I couldn't just keep him here in my shop like a princess in a tower.

But if he walked through the door, then he would go back to the future.

He might very possibly be right about the time mechanism thing.

As crazy as that sounded, it actually made sense.

"Who is that Mrs. Johnson?" he asked.

"I don't know." I shrugged. "A lady who lives in town. Her husband works at the General Store."

"She's got some nerve," Benjamin said indignantly.

"It's okay," I said. "I don't care."

He waved a hand vaguely around my shop. "If that's her fault," he said. "Then you have no choice but to care."

He was right. I did care. No matter how much I told myself I didn't care, I did.

And I knew that Mrs. Johnson as the wife of the man who ran the—established—General Store, she had some influence over the townspeople.

"Maybe," I said. "But there's nothing I can do about it."

He poured water into a glass. Seemed to consider as he drank.

"So here in 1860…"

"Nine."

"Here in 1869, what does she expect you to do?"

I sat back, straightened my skirts. It was getting cold in here. "She would expect me to get married," I said. "So I would have a man to… protect my reputation… or whatever."

He smiled a little. "Do you agree? Do you think you need to be married?"

"Maybe. I might *want* to get married. I don't *need* to get married. I can do just fine without a husband."

"You are a woman ahead of your time."

"How so?" I asked.

"You sound like a woman from the future," he said. "Women get married because they want to. Not because they have to."

"What about society? People like Mrs. Johnson?"

"Nobody cares. I don't think there are that many people like that anymore."

I rubbed my arms and shivered. "We should go sit by the fire," I said.

Benjamin took some chairs out into the shop and stoked up the fire while I went over and locked the door.

There wasn't anyone coming in anyway. We certainly didn't need any busybodies coming in sticking their nose into what we were doing.

"This is nice," he said. "You should think about leaving the chairs here like this."

"To what end?" I asked.

"For people to come here and sit. Maybe do some reading."

"Let them read for free?"

"It's a thing," he said. "People are more likely to buy something if they can read a little bit of it."

"That makes some sense, I guess". I understood it just fine. I just wasn't really interested in it right now. I was more concerned about how I was going to keep Benjamin here.

"I think I might have an idea," he said. "How to beat Mrs. Johnson at her game."

"How?"

"We'll just tell her that we're married."

"What?" The whole idea made me dizzy. "How would we do that? They all know I'm unmarried."

"So?" he asked. "How hard is it to get married around here?"

"It's not hard," I said with a little laugh.

"Do you need a license or anything?"

"I don't know. I think the preacher does all that."

"Okay," he said, leaning forward. "What do we have to do to get married? Today?"

Perhaps Benjamin wasn't from the future after all. Perhaps he had escaped from the insane asylum.

21

BENJAMIN

The snow had let up some, allowing people to move about again. The evening sunlight reflecting off the snow-capped mountains was beautiful.

This area had not changed a lot in the hundreds of years between now and then.

"I'm sorry," I said. "It was just an idea. You don't know me."

It seemed like a perfectly good idea to me, but pushing someone into a marriage they didn't want was hardly a chivalrous thing to do.

Elise pulled her shawl closer. "It's not that. I don't have to know everything about you."

"But it would help, right?"

"I suppose."

"Okay," I said. "Then I'll tell you about me."

She nodded.

"I'm from 2022. I have one sister. She's actually getting married in two days."

"She's getting married on Christmas Eve?"

"Unfortunately, yes."

"That is so romantic," she said.

"Well, she's very upset with me right now because I'm snowed in and can't get there."

"Where is the wedding?"

"In Houston," I said. "Texas."

"Oh, well," Elise said. "You couldn't possibly be there in two days anyway."

"Except that I could," I said. "If not for the weather."

"How?" She sat up. "Wait."

I watched as she went into the back, then returned with a bottle of wine and two glasses.

"I never drink," she said. "But I think I'd like a glass of wine."

I opened the wine and filled two glasses. Handed her one.

"To time," I said, echoing Vaughn's toast.

"To time." She took a sip of wine. "I'm ready now. Please tell me how you could get from here to Houston in less than two days."

I sat back. Swirled my wine a bit. I probably wasn't supposed to tell her about the future. There was probably some rule somewhere about that.

But this was my time travel and I was going to make my own rules.

"We have something called airplanes."

"Air planes."

"It's a…" I stopped and plucked a little decorative buggy off the tree. Held it out.

"It's like this."

"Okay." She smiled. "It must have really fast horses."

"No horses." I set it on the ground. "People get on it while it's on the ground. Then…" I started rolling it until it was in the air. "Then it flies. Like this."

Elise sipped her wine. "You're a teller of tall tales."

"I'm not," I said. "It's actually my job to fly these. I'm an airplane pilot. It's sort of like being a… a stage coach driver except that my coach goes in the air."

"How?"

"Even people in my time don't understand the how."

"Do you know how?" She leaned forward, holding a hand out toward the heat.

I took the poker and got the flames going again. "I know how," I said. "I'm a pilot. But please don't make me explain how. You would be asleep in five minutes."

"Okay," she said. "So how long does it take to go from here to Houston in one of your air planes?"

"About two hours."

"Hours." She sat back, gaping at me. "From weeks down to two hours."

"I know," I said. "It's pretty cool."

She smiled. "Now I know you're from the future. I've heard my sister's husband say cool."

I laughed. "What else do you want to know?"

She put a finger against her chin.

"The important things. Are you married?"

"No."

"Have you ever been married?"

"Never."

"Why not?"

"I was waiting for you."

She laughed. "My sister, Bailey, warned me about men like you."

"Like me?"

"Yes. Men with charming tongues. Men who will say anything in order to have their way with a girl."

"Is it working?" I asked. "Because if we're going to get married, I really hope I get to have my way with you."

She blushed prettily.

Then someone knocked on the door.

22

ELISE

I looked at Benjamin as the person knocked again.

"I should open the door," I said.

"Agreed," he said. "Do you want me to hide in the back?"

"Hardly. You're going to be my husband, right?"

He laughed as I unlocked the door and opened it.

Mrs. Randall stepped inside.

"Mrs. Randall," I said. "Please come in."

"Are you open?" she asked. "The door was locked. I thought maybe it was locked by mistake."

"It's a long story," I said. "Are you looking for a gift?"

"Maybe," she said. "But I actually came to see you." She glanced over at Benjamin. "Hello."

"Mrs. Randall," I said. "This is Benjamin."

"Your beau?"

"Yes," Benjamin said, standing up. Dipped his head in greeting. "It's a pleasure to meet you."

Benjamin had just told the preacher's wife that he was my beau.

"Benjamin, this is Mrs. Randall. She's the preacher's wife."

"You're kidding," he said.

"Please don't hold that against me," Mrs. Randall said. "Could I have a seat? I wanted to ask you about something."

"Please," I said. "Would you like a glass of wine?"

"No. But don't mind me." She took a seat in the chair that Benjamin had vacated and I sat next to her in the other chair.

"What did you want to talk to me about?"

She glanced over at Benjamin. "Is it okay if he hears?" She lowered her voice. "It's rather private."

"I'd like him to hear," I said. Benjamin came to stand behind my chair. He put a hand on my shoulder. An innocent gesture, really, but it sent tremors all through me and made it a little difficult to pay attention to Mrs. Randall.

"Mrs. Johnson came to see me," Mrs. Randall said, putting a hand on the arm of my chair.

"Oh no," I said, shaking my head.

All I could think was that I had invested in this shop for nothing. If the town wasn't going to support me, then there was no way I was going to be successful. I might as well just pack up and go home.

"It's okay, dear," Mrs. Randall said. "I came here to tell you. So we can figure out how to fix this."

"I know how to fix it," Benjamin said.

I turned and looked up at him along with Mrs. Randall.

"Your husband's the preacher, right?" he asked, diving in headlong.

"That's right."

Benjamin came around and sat on the arm of my chair. "Do you think he could come here? Marry us?"

I held my breath.

I couldn't believe he was asking her that. And at the same time everything seemed to hinge on Mrs. Randall's answer.

She looked from one to the other of us.

"When?" she asked.

"Now," I said, not daring to look at Benjamin. "Do you think he could come now?"

23

BENJAMIN

The clock chimed the hour. Five o'clock.

The sounds of children outside frolicking in the new fallen snow drifted inside the store.

Mrs. Randall was looking at us like we had lost our minds. I didn't blame her.

Elise and I had both gone insane. That was probably about the best explanation for what we were asking her.

"Not tonight," she said. "I know he can't come tonight." She narrowed her eyes in suspicion. "What are you two not telling me?"

"Mrs. Randall," Elise said. "You came here to tell me that Mrs. Johnson is keeping people away from my shop, right?" She sat forward. "I mean, I know what she said to me last night and now today I've had no customers."

"I just thought you should know," she said. "And thought I could help you resolve it. You have such a lovely shop here." She leaned forward and lowered her voice. "And I've no reason to put stock in any of her rumors."

"Yes," Elise said. "If Benjamin and I marry, then no one will believe whatever it is she's saying about me. Right?"

Mrs. Randall narrowed her eyes and seemed to consider. "Do you love each other?" she asked.

I took Elise's hand. "Yes."

It occurred to me that I wasn't acting rational. Something must have come over me.

But I'd been swept into a current that was taking me places I had never dreamed of. And I wanted to see where those currents went.

"Elise?" Mrs. Randall asked.

"Yes." Elise smiled and looked at me with such an intensity that it nearly took my breath away.

Mrs. Randall took a deep breath. "He can't do it tonight. Or tomorrow. He can do it day after tomorrow."

"Christmas Eve," Elise said on a whisper.

"Yes. We can do it then," she said. "Is that acceptable?"

Elise glanced at me. "Yes," she said. "It's perfect."

"Do you want us to come to your house?"

"No," Elise said quickly. "Here."

"Here?" Mrs. Randall was wavering. I could see. She sensed something wrong.

"We'd like to get married here," I said. "At Elise's new store." I squeezed Elise's hand. "It would mean a lot to her. To us."

"Very well," she said. "Mr. Randall and I will meet you two here on Christmas Eve."

Elise locked the door after Mrs. Randall left.

I stoked the fire again. Added firewood.

The weather was getting worse outside. Even now I heard wind howling around the building.

I topped off our wine, though neither of us had barely touched what was in our glasses.

"Are you sure about this?" I asked.

"Yes," she said. "You're the one I'm supposed to marry."

"No," I said. "I won't marry you just because you think we're supposed to get married."

I stared into the flames. She, too, it seemed, had been swept into a current.

But I wanted more than that.

The implications of what I was doing began to slap me in the face.

I'd be going into another time. Permanently.

I'd never see my family again.

I'd be giving up my way of life including airplanes. And nothing had ever interested me as much as aviation.

Until now. Until Elise.

But then she leaned forward and put a hand on my cheek.

"Benjamin," she said.

Then she pressed her lips against mine.

And I was lost. Just like the sirens that called the sailors onto the rocks. I was lost.

24

ELISE

The only sounds came from the saloon. Piano music and every now and then laughter would spill out onto the snow-covered streets.

Benjamin and I were on a fur blanket in front of the fireplace. I lay on my back staring up into the darkness. Benjamin sat staring into the flames.

"I met Vaughn," he said. "I talked to her."

"Who is she?"

"I think that the whole time travel thing started with her."

"I remember overhearing one of my brothers-in-law talking about a spell that flowed through their blood."

"A spell." He picked up the poker and rearranged the logs. "She said something about a spell."

"That's it then," Elise said. "You must be related to her."

"It would be so far back," he mused. "How would I know?"

She shrugged. "Do you think she knew?"

"Maybe." Benjamin lay on his back next to me. Laced his fingers loosely with mine. "If she..." He stopped.

"What?"

"I don't understand how I could be related to her if she lives in the future."

"Maybe she travels back and forth."

"Maybe," he said. "I guess you've had a lot longer to think about this than I have."

"I've had years to think about it."

I reached over and took her hands in mine. "What made you think it was me? Did I look different or something?"

"I don't know," I said. "Maybe I just wanted it to be you."

We lay in silence for a few minutes, the saloon music drifting through the air. Reflections from the fire dancing across the ceilings.

"So what if we're wrong?" he asked.

"Wrong about what?"

"Wrong about the time mechanism part."

"I don't know," I said.

"What if time has nothing to do with it," he said. "I could walk through that door at any time and never come back. Even after time passes. Even after we're married."

"Don't do that," I said.

He smiled and met my gaze in the soft firelight. "You can't keep me in here forever."

"I know. So what do we do?"

"I have an idea," he said.

"Okay."

"We'll go through the door together. Hand in hand."

"I don't know," I said. "I suppose that could work."

"You'll ground me in time. Hold me here."

"Maybe," I said.

"We have to try something."

"I know," I said. He was right. We had to try something. "After that you have to stay away from the door."

"True," he said.

"Okay. We'll try it in the morning."

"We'll tie our wrists together."

"Okay," I said. "I have lots of ribbon."

I suppose the idea was as good as any.

But I had a very bad feeling about this.

25

BENJAMIN

We woke at daybreak and started getting ready.

"I could use some coffee," I said.

"We have coffee at home," she said.

"Good," I said, helping her fasten her cloak.

I put on my hat and gloves. There were so many things wrong with this plan of ours.

Some many things that could go wrong.

Once we got through the door, I couldn't go back into her shop. Not unless we were going to do this every time. And just because it worked one time did not mean it would work every time.

She smiled at me, then went into my arms.

I held her close. So close. She smelled like wildflowers and peppermint.

"If this doesn't work," I said. "If we get separated—"

"It'll work," she said. "It has to work."

"But—"

She looked up at me. "Promise me," she said. "Promise me that tomorrow at twilight we will be married."

"Okay," I said, tucking her head back against my chest beneath my chin. "I promise."

"No matter what," she persisted.

"I promise." I kissed the top of her head. "You ready to get tied up?" I asked.

"Let's do it," she said.

She had rolls of red ribbon. It didn't take long for us to weave it around us. My left hand. Her right. Starting with our hands, I wrapped it around and around. Up our wrists. Over our elbows.

"Isn't there something called handfasting?" I asked.

"There is," she said. "An ancient ritual, I think."

"I think so, too," I said. "So in a way, we're already bound in marriage."

She smiled and I kissed her again.

"I guess it's now or never," I said.

"I don't think there is much else we can do," she said. "And we're out of firewood."

When she opened the door, the cold morning air swept inside and struck us in the face. The snow had stopped falling, but the ground was covered in white. Only a few tracks here and there where people had walked.

I ignored all the trepidation I felt. It was normal to be nervous. I was walking through a door into another way of life.

But I was with Elise. I wanted to be with her no matter when or where.

She looked at me, her eyes moist from the sting of cold air. So beautiful. Anything. I would do anything to stay with her.

Our fingers were clasped together. Our hands and arms literally tied together. This had to work.

She nodded and together we stepped through the door.

Snowflakes landed on my face. In my eyes. A sudden flurry.

I blinked against the wind whipping in my face.

It was so cold it hurt to breathe.

I looked over at Elise.

But Elise was not there.

There were no ribbons around my hand or my arm. No red ribbons anywhere.

I turned around in a complete circle, the wind biting into my face.

The streets were deserted. The traffic signals were dark from the power outage.

I stood alone on the deserted Main Street of Whiskey Springs.

I had come home.

26

ELISE

*I*n the dim early morning light, I saw the tendrils of mist hanging low over the street. The saloon was quiet this early in the morning. Everything was quiet.

The red ribbon Benjamin had so carefully wrapped around our arms and our hands fluttered off my wrist to drag on the ground.

I lifted my right arm. It was like Benjamin had never been there.

Turning, I went back inside my shop and knelt on the fur rug, my skirts belling out around me.

Our plan had not worked.

We had walked through the door. Bound, hand-in-hand. But he had walked back into the future, leaving me behind.

"Why?"

We were supposed to be getting married.

In some ways we were already married. Handfasted.

In my heart I was married to him.

He had known. He had known this might not work. But I had insisted that it had to.

Even being bound together could not keep us in the same time.

It was hopeless.

He was in the future and I was in the past.

The only way he could stay in the past was to stay in my shop.

What was the point? It was pointless.

What was the point of him coming to the past? Of us falling in love only to be separated by a door?

I suddenly hated my shop.

I hated everything about it.

I would just close it up. Let the hateful people—the Mrs. Johnsons—have it. I didn't want to even live here without Benjamin.

Taking a deep, ragged breath, I straightened and pulled myself together.

He and I had a promise. He would come back.

Tomorrow. He would come back and we would be married. By Mr. Randall. A real wedding.

That would keep us together.

It had to. It had to work.

Standing up, I decided I would just go home, clean up, and change clothes. Maybe talk Hector into heating enough water for me to have a hot bath. Then I would come back here. I would come back here and wait for him.

He had promised. He would come back to me.

He had to. Believing it was the only way my heart could bear it.

Without the belief that he would come back, I had nothing.

Stepping back out into the cold, alone this time, I walked home. Alone.

I was about halfway home, still holding the red ribbon, when Eamon came up behind me and fell into step alongside me.

"Hello Elise," he said.

I wasn't in the mood to talk to Eamon. I wasn't in the mood to talk to anyone.

He blocked my path and grabbed hold of my arms.

"Stop it," I pulled away, more annoyed than afraid. Shook his hands off me.

"What? I'm not good enough for you? *He's* the only one good enough to keep you warm at night?" He took my arms again, this time, more forcefully.

"What are you talking about? What are you doing?" I was again struck by how his scent reminded me of a wet goat.

"I'm taking you home with me."

"No," I screeched, trying to pull away, but his grip was strong. Too strong for me to fight against.

He put something over my mouth. I fought against him, but he was too strong. I scratched at his face with my nails. Pushed at his face, scratching him with my fingertips, but I was losing strength fast.

Then everything went black.

27

BENJAMIN

*W*ith the wind howling around me and the snow blinding me, I walked up and down the street several times.

Each time I stopped at the door to Elise's shop and tried the door. I looked in the window. The little train sat on its tracks its own little imaginary town. Tried the door again And again.

But I found no indication whatsoever that the past had ever existed.

After one more fruitless shove at the Timeless Keepsakes door, I gave up and walked back to the bed and breakfast.

I was the only person out this early on this frozen morning.

The walk didn't take long.

I went inside, closing the door firmly behind me.

"There you are," Marshall said. "Missed you last night."

I mumbled something incoherent. It might have been more of a growl. I didn't know and I didn't care.

I went upstairs, closed my door, and stood in the cold, dark bedroom.

Freezing to death was not going to solve anything.

I made a fire in the fireplace and sat down in the chair in front of it.

I'm not sure how long I sat there staring into the flames.

I thought about nothing. And somehow everything.

There was no way to fix this.

No logical way to fix this.

I was at a loss.

I rubbed my left hand where the red ribbon had been tied.

Elise and I had for all intents and purposes been handfasted.

To me, that meant we were married.

I was in the future. My wife in the past.

Finally, I got up and prowled my bedroom like a caged animal.

Then I left my room and went downstairs. Wandered into the kitchen.

Marshall silently handed me a mug of coffee. I stood at the window, watching the winter storm rage outside. Drank the coffee, not even tasting it.

I heard Marshall moving about behind me.

He somehow knew to say nothing.

I left the kitchen. Paced around the parlor. Stood at the closed door.

There was no reason to try to go back out. Not right now.

I wanted to. I fought against the instinct to run back out to the shop like a man possessed.

Instead I went back up to my room and changed clothes. There was no water for a shower, but putting on dry clothes helped.

Then my gaze landed on the letter on my nightstand. My name was scrawled across the front. My hands shaking, I opened the letter and started to read it a second time.

DEAR BENJAMIN,

I know you had to go. That you had no choice.
I'll just say it. Please come back.
If you believe... If you believe in us...
Meet me at the park at Twilight tonight. Christmas Eve.
I'll be there. Waiting for you.
No matter when. I'll be there.
Please don't leave me here without you.
Yours forever,
Elise

ELISE HAD WRITTEN this note to me hundreds of years ago. And somehow it had survived. Not only had it survived, but it had ended up in my hands.

Right here. Right now.

She was real.

And she was waiting for me.

I wanted to race back to her shop. To force my way back in time.

But I forced myself to maintain my composure.

I needed to think.

I needed to figure this out before I did anything rash. I needed to learn more before I went back. I needed to find answers.

My phone was dead, so I had no Internet.

With no Internet at my disposal, I went into the library and began digging through books.

Finally, I found a book that caught my attention

Lavender Blue. Auclair.

It was a basically a photo book containing Bailey Auclair's paintings. Elise's sister.

I took it with me out to the fireplace and sat down.

With a purpose now, I began to settle.

I opened the book and started on page one.

28

ELISE

*W*hen I woke, everything hurt. I was lying on a bed. Not my bed. A bed that smelled… weird.

I had a metallic taste in my dry mouth and my ears were ringing.

When I tried to roll over, I discovered that my wrists were bound. Not with a soft red ribbon. But with a rough rope. A rope that dug into my skin when I tugged at it.

I turned over anyway.

In a darkened room, I only saw shadows.

The outline of a four-poster bed. The outline of a dresser. A wardrobe.

It looked like a lady's room. But not mine.

Not one that I had ever seen before.

I heard a noise coming from somewhere in the house. A banging. Like a blacksmith making horseshoes.

I lay very still. Forced myself to remember.

The last thing I remembered was standing with Benjamin as he tied our hands and wrists together.

We'd been handfasted. Or close enough to count.

As far as I was concerned, Benjamin was my husband.

We'd walked through the door.

But we had been separated.

My head pounded as I tried to think.

I needed to think. I needed to remember everything.

Benjamin had gone back to the future then. He had left me here. Alone.

I had been walking home.

Heartbroken.

Then… Eamon had grabbed my arm.

He had done something.

Fear shot through me.

Eamon had tied me up. I was in his house.

As I lay there listening to someone moving around the house where I was a prisoner, I cursed Mrs. Johnson.

He comes from a good family. But I haven't met them.

Eamon may have come from a good family, but he was not a good man.

I barely breathed when the door opened and he crossed the room, his boots landing heavy across the wooden floor to the bed.

As he stood over me, I counted to ten. Barely breathing. Then counted to ten again.

"I know you're awake," he said. "You need to drink something."

He lifted my head as he stuck a glass up to my lips. I reluctantly drank. If I didn't he was going to pour the water or whatever it was all over me.

"Get your strength back," he said. "When you wake up, I expect the same treatment you gave that yokel." He walked off, slammed the door behind him. Clicking a lock into place.

I wanted to scream at him. Benjamin was not a yokel. He was my husband.

But I couldn't get my lips to work. And I knew better than to say anything to him anyway.

So I lay there in the dark. Beneath the smelly wool blanket.

When the tears fell down my cheeks, I didn't even try to stop them.

Eamon was somewhere in the house whistling to himself now.

He was an insane man.

He had no right to kidnap me like this.

I tugged at my wrists, but they were tied too tight.

I tugged too hard and felt the dampness of blood.

No one knew where I was. I didn't even know where I was.

29

BENJAMIN

*S*ince it consisted mostly of pictures, I didn't take me long to get through the entire book.

There were photos in the back though. Pictures of Bailey's family including one of the whole family

But Elise was not in it.

In fact, I didn't see her name listed anywhere.

I checked again, but Elise was not in the book with the rest of her family.

"Why?" I asked out loud.

She owned her own shop in the town of Whiskey Springs. A businesswoman. She should be in her sister's book. Even better, she should have her own book.

With my phone charged up, I went to the Internet.

Elise Auclair.

I got a couple of hits on Facebook. Added Whiskey Springs. Nothing. Added the 1800s. Nothing.

She could not have simply vanished from the face of the earth.

A door slammed upstairs.

I ignored it. I didn't have time for riddles right now.

Vaughn came to stand next to me.

"Benjamin," she said. "Elise is in trouble."

"What?" My phone clattered to the floor as I stood up. "HOW do you know this? WHAT do you know?"

"Please," she said. Her voice was kind. Soothing. "Sit. I'll explain."

I sat down.

"I'll give you the short version of the explanation," she said. "My daughter Anna has learned how to control, at least somewhat, my time travel." She held up a hand. "No one else's. Not even hers. I'm the only one who carries the original spell. The rest of you carry a diluted version."

"The rest of us?"

"You're my great great... great... maybe great... great nephew or something. I don't keep up with all that. Anna knows. I don't want to know. It just makes me feel old."

I smiled and almost laughed. "You're Miss Dupre," I said. "From the story."

"Vaughn Dupre Becquerel."

Vaughn had such a calming presence about her. I wondered if it had something to do with the spell or maybe that she had been born in the 1700s. Then I occurred to me that she was being disarming on purpose. To put me at ease.

"Elise," I said. "She's not in this book."

"No." A shadow crossed Vaughn's face. "She is at a crossroads. She needs you."

"What kind of crossroads?" I asked, my voice husky with fear.

"One that determines whether or not she's ultimately in this book."

"How?" I struggled to keep my voice steady. "How can I help her when I'm here?"

"I'm going to help you with that," she said.

30

ELISE

*W*hatever Eamon had done to me had worn off by the next morning.

Christmas Eve morning.

It surprised me when he untied me.

"I have to go out for a bit," he said. "You stay here."

"No," I said, standing up. "I'm going home."

He shoved me back onto the bed. I landed hard, but immediately sat up.

"You'll be here when I get back," he said, standing over me. "And we'll celebrate Christmas." He leaned close. Leering. So close I could smell his rancid breath.

I wanted him away from me. That was all I could think. *Get away.*

Without thinking, I slapped him on the cheek.

That's when he hit me. He really hit me. With his fist.

"Don't ever do that again," he said, turning on his heels and walking to the door. I heard the lock turn behind him.

I gently touched my lip. It was bleeding. He'd hit me hard enough to bust my lip.

I blinked back the tears, reached deep, and found survival instinct instead.

After checking each of the two windows and the door, I accepted that I was locked in.

I went back to one of the windows and forced myself to think.

I was on the third floor of a house. No balcony.

Mrs. Johnson had said Eamon didn't live far from her. So I must be west of town.

I reserved the option of busting a window and jumping out. That option was there if I didn't come up with anything better in the next little bit.

Eamon would be back. He said he had to go out *for a bit*. It was hard to say just how long *a bit* was.

I just knew I had to be out of here before he got back.

I checked the room for something that would break out a window.

I found nothing.

Pacing the room, I knew I was in trouble. As much as I wanted it to be an option, I knew I could not survive a jump from the third floor. Eamon knew that, too.

That was why he had left me here.

At least he had left a fire going for me. So considerate, I thought sarcastically.

I lay back down on the bed and forced myself to think rationally.

First of all, would anyone be looking for me? Hector, maybe. But probably not. He tended to stay out of my personal affairs.

Colton, maybe. I never knew if he was going to be home or not. But it was Christmas. He was usually home on Christmas. Or with one of my sisters.

I honestly did not know. I did know that I couldn't count on anyone coming to look for me.

Not even my handfasted husband Benjamin. He was in the future. Not even he could help me.

No one would worry when I didn't open the shop this morning. They'd think I was taking Christmas Eve off. Or that I had closed down. It wasn't like anyone had come in yesterday anyway, what with Mrs. Johnson spewing poison about me.

So that meant I was on my own.

I had no weapon.

No way to get off the third floor of the house.

I closed my eyes.

I'd think of something. I had to.

A few minutes later I got up to stir the fire.

I turned the poker over in my hands.

I had been wrong. I did have a weapon. And if I kept it hot, it would be all the better.

Sitting on the floor in front of the fire, I got the pointed end of the poker nice and hot.

Now all I had to was to wait.

Now that I had a plan, Eamon's luck had run out.

A little later, I'm not sure how much later, I heard a door open downstairs.

Then I heard the footsteps of someone coming up the stairs. The occasional creak of old wooden stairs.

I wrapped my fingers around the poker.

Eamon didn't know me very well. He was in for a surprise.

31

BENJAMIN

I walked through the door to Timeless Keepsakes into a dark room. It was different without Elise here. I didn't like it.

The only sounds drifted in from outside. Piano music from the saloon. A horse and wagon rumbling along the road.

The shop smelled like a peppermint evergreen tree. I hadn't really noticed that before when I'd been so focused on Elise. But now, like everything else, the scent reminded me of her.

Vaughn had powers other people didn't have.

She hadn't told me *how* she knew things. Just that she did.

It didn't even matter how.

What mattered was that I do what she said and find Elise.

If I didn't find Elise, she wasn't going to live to be in that photograph in her sister's book.

I was pretty sure I was about to tear this town apart to find her.

No matter what it took, I would do it.

The first thing I had to do was to get out of here.

Vaughn had been very specific, leaving nothing to chance.

I picked up the fireplace poker and took it with me into the back room to stand in front of the window. Vaughn had said the back window, not the window next to the front door.

It was rather odd that it had not occurred to either Elise or me to consider this window.

Don't worry about the destruction, she had said. *Just bust it out.*

I hefted the poker over my shoulder like a baseball bat, then slammed it against the glass.

With a sound that could be heard across town, the window shattered. Glass and splintered wood went everywhere.

Compared to windows of the future, it wasn't very sturdy.

Using my gloved hands, I knocked out the rest of the glass and window panes.

The window was about four feet by six feet. Plenty big for me to crawl through.

I hefted myself up, then landed on my feet on the ground on the other side of the window.

Looking around, I held my breath, willing Vaughn to be right that this would work.

Since I was behind the shop, I really didn't know. Music from saloon was a good sign. I think the saloon was closed down in the future, but if anything opened up in a winter storm, it would be the saloon.

I walked around the building and let out a sigh of relief.

A carriage pulled by four horses rumbled past. Two young boys rolled a big circle with a stick.

No street lights. No motorized vehicles.

It was a welcome idyllic scene. It had worked.

I was in the past.

Vaughn had been a little less clear on the next part. She only knew specifics about the time travel. She didn't know exactly where I would find Elise.

So I went against every man code and stepped into the saloon to ask for directions to her house. Then I asked about the Johnson house. No reason other than a feeling.

"The Johnson house?" the bartender said. "Of course." He pointed west. "Just outside of town. That way."

Maybe the man code had not been established yet.

Thinking it didn't make sense that Elise would be in trouble in her own home, I headed west toward the Johnson house.

I walked slowly, taking in everything. I didn't know what I was looking for. Anything that didn't add up.

Vaughn had suggested that something had happened to Elise on her way home. She didn't know what. But my guess was the she had never made it home.

I walked beneath huge trees. Pine. Spruce. Fir. All covered in icicles and a layer of snow. The road was little more than a trail.

The Johnsons had their name on a little wooden sign on their white picket fence, so I kept going.

Following my gut.

A man on horseback came from an old tall three-story house sitting off half-hidden in the trees.

I stepped behind a large spruce tree and waited for him to pass.

The man looked familiar. I'd seen him before. In Elise's shop.

And that's when I saw it. The red ribbon we had used to tie ourselves together, ground into the dirt. It was filthy, but I picked it up and stashed it in my pocket.

I was on the right track.

My heart pounding fast, I made my way to the door.

It wasn't locked, so I pushed it open and stepped inside.

The putrid smell—like rotten potatoes—was so strong, I nearly turned around and went back outside into the fresh air.

But I needed to check for Elise. She could be here. The man who had been in her shop could have her here.

I checked the first floor, then went up to the second. No sign of her.

Just a filthy house. Dirty clothes strewn everywhere. Plates with half-eaten meals. It was a pig sty.

The thought of Elise being anywhere near here made my blood run cold and I slowly made my way up the next set of stairs.

Three of the steps were broken and I had to step carefully over them. When one of the steps cracked under my weight, I decided this part of the house must not ever be used anymore.

I was wasting my time here.

32

ELISE

*W*hen I left the poker in the fire, it heated not only the tip, but the whole thing. I ripped a good-sized strip off the end of my petticoat and wrapped it around the poker to keep it from burning my hands.

Hoping I could keep my grip on it, I went to stand behind the door and contemplated how I was going to defend myself against Eamon. Would it be better to strike him on the head or run him through with it?

It was quite possible that I didn't have the strength to really do either and since I had no experience in such things, I decided to just strike him with the hot end. Besides, I really didn't want to kill him.

I just wanted to get away from him.

As his footsteps neared the door, I considered doing none of the above and just running.

I had arranged the blankets and pillow so that at first glance it looked like I was in the bed.

As the locked turned, I decided that was what I would do. I would simply hide behind the door, then run like the devil while he walked toward the bed.

I would use the poker only as needed.

My mouth was dry and I swallowed hard. Watched the doorknob turn.

This was it.

It was Christmas Eve. He had promised that tonight was the night for his nefarious activity.

It was now or never.

The door slowly opened. Standing behind the door, I held my breath as he stepped inside and started across the room.

He didn't see me.

As he reached the bed, I ducked around the door and ran. My skirt caught on a splinter in the door and it ripped, but I just kept going.

I hit the steps hard, not looking back.

One of the steps broke under my weight and I barely caught myself.

I kept going, running blindly. I reached the second floor before I heard him coming after me.

As I ran down the second-floor hallway, still holding the hot poker, I looked back over my shoulder, but I didn't see him. I kept running.

Just as I turned back around, knowing I had to be close to the second staircase, I ran headlong into Eamon.

I knew it was him. I could tell by his smell. Enough like a wet goat that I immediately recognized him.

I swung my hot poker, but it was too late. He already had me pinned against him.

"How did you get out, you little wrench?"

I could barely catch my breath.

How could there be two of him?

My poker clattered to the floor. But it didn't stop me from defending myself. I scratched every body part of his I could reach. I even had myself a handful of his hair before he pinned my arms down.

I was blinded by fear and survival.

"I think it's time you learned a lesson or two." He lifted me off my feet and, instead of carrying me back up the stairs to the third floor, he dragged me into a second-story room.

He dropped me onto a bed, knocking the breath out of me. All I could do was wait for the next onslaught.

There was a noise. God only knows what that was.

Then he landed on top of me. The wet goat smell was overwhelming.

I screamed and struggled to get away, but he simply fell off me, landing hard on the floor.

"Elise."

I covered my head and squeezed my eyes closed. "No."

"Elise."

I lay very still.

"It's me. Benjamin."

Slowly opening my eyes, I turned over and sat up. My hands were fisted and trembling.

It was Benjamin.

Eamon lay sprawled on the floor.

I stepped over him and threw myself into Benjamin's arms.

He kissed the top of my head.

"Let's get out here before he comes to."

He took me by the hand and together we left the old house.

33

BENJAMIN

The Auclair house was the same but different.

I sat in front of the fireplace holding a glass filled with strong whiskey.

The fireplace was the same. If I stared into the flames, I couldn't tell which time period I was in.

The grandfather clock was the same. Stood in the same place next to the stairs, steadily ticking away the minutes. Not caring if the minutes were in 1869 or 2022.

The furniture was different, but not significantly so. Since the power had been out in the future, the house seemed more alike than different to me.

Hector, a man Elise called the butler, had served us dinner while he heated water for her bath.

He barely blinked an eye when she led me into the kitchen. He was, however, concerned with her disheveled appearance and busted lip.

A raised eyebrow in my direction was about as far as that got before Elise put that to rest.

The whiskey helped dull some of the anger boiling inside

me. Elise and I had reported the incident to the sheriff. A fellow by the name of Jeb. Jeb said he would take care of it and I believed him.

But every time I looked at Elise's busted lip, I wanted to go back out there and tear Eamon to shreds. He deserved to pulled apart limb by limb as far as I was concerned.

But, of course, I maintained my civility and allowed the law to run its course.

It was snowing outside again.

Beautiful soft flakes floating down.

Christmas Eve snow was magical. I'd always believed that. And I believed it now.

Against all odds, I had gone back in time.

It had been with Vaughn Becquerel's help. If it hadn't been for her, Elise would not have survived.

Needing something else to think about, I got up and wandered around the parlor.

Elegantly lit by flickering candles, it felt like home.

I stopped at the bottom of the stairs and looked up. I needed to talk to Elise.

She needed to know that her shop had a broken window.

I had an idea how to fix the problem with the front door being my portal into the future, but first we had some things to do.

Not the least of which was a wedding.

Hundreds of years in the future, my sister was getting married right now. She would never know that I was getting married on Christmas Eve in the past.

The only way she would find out would be for her to do some research. First of all, that wasn't her style. She was a here and now kind of girl. And second, she would always just believe that I had simply disappeared.

Maybe I could find a way to send her a message. There was

no hurry. That could wait. Right now I had the love of my life to focus on.

I had just settled back in front of the fireplace when a man walked through the front door.

He was a handsome man. About Elise's age.

Dressed quite formally, he took off his hat and handed it to Hector who also took his coat.

The man and Hector spoke in low tones before the man walked over to me.

"You're Benjamin," he said.

"Benjamin Smith." I stood up and held out my hand.

"I'm Colton Auclair," he said, shaking my hand. "I've just come from town and there are about a million rumors going around right about now about you and my sister."

"I can only imagine," I said, sitting back down.

"Since you're here in our home drinking our whiskey, I choose to believe the one that says you saved her life."

I glanced at the amber liquid in my glass. "You would be right."

Colton slid into the other chair. "I met that Eamon fellow once," he said. "Got bad vibes off him."

"Bad vibes?" That was an expression I never expected to come out of a nineteenth century man's mouth.

"I've spent some time with my three brothers-in-law," he said, with a little smile. "Anyway, my sister tried to talk to me about you, but I wouldn't listen to her."

"I guess it didn't make much sense."

Colton stretched out his long legs. "It made perfect sense," he said. "But I didn't want her to get her hopes up about a stranger she just met."

"It's good that she's got you to watch out for her," I said.

Colton scoffed. "I think you hold that distinction. You're the one who saved her life today."

"Well," I said. "That fellow, Eamon is lucky I'm a law-abiding citizen. Else he would have found his own body parts scattered from here to hell and back."

"We'll reserve that as an option for later," Colton said.

I laughed. I liked Elise's brother already. "Just say the word."

"There's another rumor," Colton said. "If it's true, I guess you and I need to have a different discussion."

34

ELISE

I stayed in the tub of hot water until it cooled off, which, quite honestly, wasn't nearly long enough. But I was clean. No lingering wet goat smell remaining.

I dried off in front of the fire and decided that since it was Christmas Eve I'd wear my new red dress. I'd never even tried it on.

My sister Bailey had sent it to me a couple of months ago. After admiring the formal dress with a million miles of red velvet used to make the skirts, I had put it away in my wardrobe as one of those things I would never have occasion to wear.

But today I did.

Today was my wedding day.

On Christmas Eve.

So it seemed like a fitting time to wear it.

It took some time to get dressed by myself. My sister Bailey had ladies to help her dress every day.

Today I missed them. My three sisters.

But I quickly put aside my sadness. They were living their lives and I had every right to live mine.

So I sat down and brushed out my hair, letting it dry from the heat of the fireplace before I pulled it up off my face, keeping a few tendrils free to frame my face. I worked quickly to make myself presentable. With three sisters, I'd had plenty of experience with hair and such.

I heard my brother's voice drift up from downstairs, then heard him laugh. Colton and Benjamin. Their laughter filled my heart.

I could put the horrendous events of the day that involved Eamon aside and focus on the good parts.

Benjamin and I were about to be married. To be really married.

Even Colton hadn't believed me about Benjamin.

But I had known the moment I saw him that he was the one.

He'd asked me how I knew.

My pulse had skittered into a thousand different directions when I'd seen him. An instant attraction.

Even if he hadn't been from the future, I know I still would have fallen in love with him at first sight.

He did look different though. He had a similar look to my brothers-in-law. A modern, confident look.

Clean-shaven and short hair, I thought with a smile, that I was drawn to.

Hearing a commotion downstairs, I put on my shoes and left my room.

Reaching the top of the stairs, I stood for a moment.

Benjamin stood there, resting an elbow on the banister.

My heart did some funny little flips that I would probably never get used to.

He looked up when he saw me and smiled up at me.

He was definitely the one.

One hand on the banister, the other used to maneuver my skirts, I carefully made my way downstairs.

He kissed me on the cheek.

"I have a surprise for you," he said. "but first I have to take care of something."

"Okay," I said, looking from him to Colton and back again.

He tucked my hand in the crook of his elbow and led me to the fireplace to take a seat on the couch.

"You look awful," Colton said.

"Thank you."

"I'm just grateful you're okay," he added.

Whatever I was going to say back to my brother was quickly forgotten as Benjamin knelt in front of me.

"Elise Auclair," he said. "You've had my heart since the moment I first saw you."

My eyes misted over as I realized he was proposing to me. Officially. With my brother as witness.

"It matters not what time we live in as long as we can spend our lives together. I don't have much… anything… to offer you right now, but I'll figure something out."

"I'm not worried about that," I said.

He smiled and kissed the back of my hand.

"Elise," he said. "Will you marry me?"

"Yes," I said. "I'll marry you. Again. On one condition."

"What's that, love?"

"Don't ever walk through that door again."

"I have some ideas about that," he said. "You don't have to worry."

35

BENJAMIN

Our wedding took place at twilight in front of a lovely Colorado blue spruce in what would one day be Auclair Memorial Park.

I didn't tell anyone, of course, that this section of town would one day be dedicated to the Auclair family.

The row of blue spruce trees provided a background in front of a background.

The setting sunlight splashed a rainbow of colors on the mountaintops behind the trees.

The preacher, Mr. Randall was there with his wife.

Both of them were very gracious.

I could not have asked for anything more.

And Elise... Elise was more beautiful than words.

Her long velvet red dress contrasted with the white snow. She looked like a princess.

Snow White, I decided.

I barely even noticed her busted lip, but when I kissed her, I gently kissed her on the other side of her mouth.

To me, the busted lip served as a reminder that it was my job to keep her safe.

To ward off anyone who might want to hurt her for whatever reason.

As we gathered in front of the tree with Mr. and Mrs. Randall, other people found their way over, too.

Soon we were surrounded by townspeople. All smiling, some crying tears of happiness.

Elise, noticing them, made a comment about the tears.

"We make a beautiful couple," I said. "It brings people to tears."

She smiled. "I know."

"The townspeople are holding a reception at the saloon for us," I said. "Do you want to go?"

She shrugged. "Probably should. Since we're shop owners and all."

"I thought you might say that."

"What's your solution about the portal?" she asked as we walked hand in hand toward the saloon.

"You'll see," I said. "Did I mention that you have to replace the back window?"

She smiled. "Colton already boarded it up."

"I know," I said. "The Auclair family is quite impressive."

"Yes," she said. "But now I'm a Smith."

"Yes. You are. Are you okay with that? Because if you're not..."

"Stop it," she said. "I consider myself a modern woman and all, but I'm not too modern to take my husband's name. Besides, what would our children call themselves?"

I just smiled. I didn't need to tell her just how complicated that could get to be.

Right now I was happy as a lark. And the problems of future generations did not concern me. As far as I was concerned, they could work out their own issues.

When we stepped into the saloon, the wedding music started. Someone was playing the wedding march on the piano.

The townspeople cheered as we walked in.

Bottles of champagne popped and the music soon changed to a happy waltz.

"Do you know how to waltz?" she asked, leaning close.

"As a matter of fact..." I pulled her into a waltz.

As we swept around the room, her full ballgown belling around her, my heart nearly burst with joy.

It was beautiful here. I liked the people—most of them, at least. There were bad people no matter the time and place, but overall there were good people here.

Elise—my new bride—and I were going to be happy.

Married at twilight.

Together forever.

EPILOGUE

Elise

One year later
Christmas Eve

It was one of those moderate seasons, so far at least. It was cold, but not unbearably so.

Snowflakes fluttered downward landing softly on the cool ground.

A red cardinal came to sit on the windowsill. I sat very still and watched it watch me. It sat there for several minutes before it spread its wings and flew off.

A cardinal in winter was a sign of good luck, so they said.

If I had any more good luck, I wasn't sure what I would do with it. I was already bursting with happiness.

I had enough warm wax to make another batch of dipped pinecones.

With plenty of silver ones and enough red ones for now—there were never enough red ones this year, it was time for a decision.

Blue or green.

Green, being a popular Christmas color was the logical choice. But instead, I went with blue.

I had a couple of reasons for that. Blue and silver went really well together. Better, really, than red and silver. Maybe next year, I'd decorate in blue and silver on my own tree.

As a shop owner, I needed to offer as many colors as possible. Red. Silver. Blue. Green.

But I'd save the green for next year.

I had another reason for picking blue.

I'd experimented some with red in an attempt to make pink. I was a little disappointed in the results. I wasn't giving up though.

If there was a need, I'd try again later.

I mixed in the blue color, working to get it just right. Added just a little more color.

Then I had it. Baby blue wax.

I hummed to myself as I lost myself in making baby blue wax coated pinecones.

The sounds of piano music drifted from the saloon down the street with children's laughter mixed in.

I kept the shop open just in case someone needed a last minute Christmas gift, but it seemed everyone had what they needed already.

I looked up when the door to the shop opened and Benjamin stepped inside.

"Did you get what you needed?" I asked.

"More or less," he said, bending over to kiss me firmly on the lips.

He sat in a chair and held out his gloved hands toward the flames in the fireplace.

"About ready to go home?" he asked.

"Almost. Just a half dozen more and I'll be finished."

"What's with the blue?" he asked.

I smiled. As far as he knew, I'd never made any wax pinecones with anything other than red and silver wax except for one time when I'd tried some green. He didn't know about the pink.

I shrugged.

"And you know it's Christmas Eve..." he said.

I knew what he was thinking. And he was right for the most part. The Christmas season was over. Yet here I sat making more of what we considered Christmas decorations.

"Wax pinecones aren't just for Christmas anymore," I said.

"Is that so?" he asked.

"I'm thinking they can be for decorating all year long. Spring... Summer... Parlors..."

"Right," he said, staring absently into the flames.

"Nurseries," I added.

He nodded. Then he turned and looked at me with a strange expression.

I smiled to myself and began straightening up my work station.

"Are you trying to tell me something?" he asked.

"Well... Mr. Smith," I said. "I might be."

He came over and pulled me to my feet.

"We're having a baby?" he asked.

I nodded. "Are you happy?"

He pulled me close enough to pick me off my feet and twirled me around.

"I could not be happier."

A sound from the front window caught our attention and we froze.

"What is that?" I asked, looking alarmed toward the shop's front window.

"I'm not sure," he said, taking my hand and we slowly walked toward the window.

It sounded like nothing I had ever heard. And bright lights flickered from outside.

We stood there. Side by side. Looking out the window.

There were sparkling white lights on hundreds of poles. Strung across the street. And bright lights coming from buggies. Horseless, roaring buggies traveling quickly up and down the road.

There was loud music coming from somewhere. Discordant music with someone singing like I had never heard before.

I could only stare out at the scene. Spellbound.

Then it stopped.

Just as suddenly as it had appeared.

There was nothing out the window other than the snowy, deserted street.

I blinked. Not daring to move.

"Benjamin?" I asked, gripping his hand like a vise to make sure he was still there. "What was that?"

Pulling me close, he pressed a hand against my flat stomach.

"We just had a glimpse into the future," he said. "The baby's future."

"But...?"

He smiled into my eyes. "Our baby carries my blood," he said. "So our blood is mixed now."

I gasped.

"We saw the future?"

"Yes," he said. "I think we saw a glimpse."

He kissed me on the forehead. "Happy anniversary, love."

ANOTHER EPILOGUE

People gathered at Twilight on Christmas Eve in 2022 to perhaps catch a glimpse of the ghost of Elise Auclair.

They waited as the sun splattered an array of color across the snow-covered peaks. They waited a little bit longer... just in case.

The weather was cold. Only those of heartiest determination stayed until the darkness of night overshadowed any hint of twilight.

Elise did not show herself that night.

In fact, she was never seen again.

Those who were fortunate to see her in 2021 were the last to see the ghost of Elise Auclair.

They soon stopped coming. There was no need.

According to the legend, she had been waiting for her one true love to come back through time for her.

Then, after all those hundreds of years, he did.

Benjamin Smith and Elise Auclair, the first owners of Timeless Keepsakes were finally together.

And time wove itself together like there had never been so much as a gap.

A small little shop that grew into an iconic gift shop and coffee shop all in one.

The shop had no front door. Only a back door with seating spilling outside into a brick walled area with two firepits that were always going.

The front of the store had just one long display window.

It was said that the front door was a portal through time.

Of course, the logical people—those with no imagination—claimed it was merely a ploy to steal customers away from the General Store.

Whatever the purpose, the little shop came alive with hauntingly festive music and sparkling lights at Twilight on Christmas Eve. It only happened for an instant.

Maybe someone saw it. Maybe they didn't.

But it happened. A coming together of past and future.

For better or for worse.

Keep Reading for a preview of MOUNTBATTEN PINK...

MOUNTBATTEN PINK PREVIEW

Chapter 1
Isabella Becquerel

Today

*M*E: *I'm here.*
        After texting Thomas, I tucked my phone into the pocket of my long light brown wool coat.

"This is it," the cab driver said with a thick accent.

"This is what?" I asked, looking out the windows for any sign of the Daniels House hotel.

"You wait here for carriage," he said in what he obviously thought was for clarification.

I shook my head and made no move to open the door.

The cab driver watched me in the rearview mirror for about five seconds, then got out and opened my door.

"There's nothing here," I insisted, not budging.

"Carriage Stop," he said, leaving the door open and going around to open the trunk. He pulled out my two big suitcases and set them on the ground.

"No... Ugh." Bringing my leather laptop messenger bag and my LV handbag with me, I slid out of the cab.

The driver rolled my luggage over to what he called the Carriage Stop, then circled back to close my door.

"Have good trip," he said, getting into the driver's seat and driving off. I watched the cab's brake lights as he followed the sharp downhill curve and disappeared the way we had just come.

A burst of cold wind, coming off rugged Rocky Mountain peaks towering in every direction swept through the valley.

My messenger bag over one shoulder, my handbag over the other, I held onto my burgundy cloche hat and turned my back to the wind.

The cab driver had left me here in the middle of nowhere. I had booked him to take me to the Daniels House hotel. Not to leave me—and my two bags of luggage—on the side of the road.

I'll take care of this. I'll just report him. I took my phone out of my pocket and unlocked it.

No service.

Seriously? I had just texted Thomas. I pulled up his message. *Message not delivered.*

I was literally out here alone with no cell phone service.

Turning, I glared at the wooden bench serving as what looked more like a resting stop in a park than a bus stop.

I sat on the cold bench and crossed my arms, choosing mad over scared.

June in the mountains of Colorado was a lot colder than I expected. It had been sweltering hot for months already in

Houston. And to think I had only brought my coat because Thomas told me about a hundred times that I would need it.

He was right about that. But I was not convinced that he was right that this trip was a good idea.

Ten months of face-time calls, texts, and emails after three years of dating.

He'd followed a new job from Houston to San Francisco and I had stayed in Houston where I had a perfectly good office and a long waiting list of clients.

I'd asked Thomas to come visit me in Houston. Offered to visit him in San Francisco.

But… no. I liked to consider myself flexible, so I'd gone along with this trip to Colorado.

It'll be fun.

You'll love it.

It's beautiful.

I had translated that into romantic. Figured we would decide what we were going to do about our relationship. We couldn't keep going like this. Not seeing each other for ten months.

Our holiday trip had fallen through. Something to do with his sister.

It wasn't a huge deal. The holidays had been a busy time of year for me, too, so I had let it slide.

Thomas and I had been together for three years, starting in college. We had a history together. That was supposed to mean something.

I looked off to my left. The Daniels House was supposed to be right up the road, tucked at the top of the mountains in a nest of fir and spruce trees. They touted unparalleled views. Exquisite cuisine. Personalized service.

Maybe I would just walk the rest of the way. I did not need a carriage to take me to the hotel. I adjusted my bags, grabbed a suitcase with each hand and took five steps.

They could have sprung a bit to make themselves a decent road. The road was nothing more than a wide walking path. No wonder they didn't allow cars up here. They didn't want the liability.

I was wearing boots, but city hiking boots, not country hiking boots.

This was not going to work.

I looked over my shoulder. There were snow clouds coming in.

The only reason I knew this was because I had visited my brother in Salt Lake City for Christmas two years ago. Instead of a mild Texas holiday, I had experienced a winter storm that had delayed my flight home for three days.

I was just about to turn back when I saw two horses and a wagon coming my way.

I pulled my suitcases to the side of the road and grabbed my hat before another gust of wind blew it away. It whipped at my long skirt beneath my coat and I wished that I had worn something warmer.

I watched the horse and wagon slowly approach. Someone was terribly confused about what a carriage was. This was a wagon. The kind people used in the western movies.

The driver, wearing a heavy coat and hat, stopped just after the two horses passed me.

"Hello," he said, tipping his hat at me.

"Hi," I said, holding my own hat to keep it from flying off, and looking up at the ruggedly handsome man with gritty stubble. If he was going for the dangerous western gunslinger look, he had it pegged.

He was grinning at me and for some reason, that irritated me.

Chapter 2

Colton Auclair

1870

THERE WAS a storm coming and being the only single man on what we'd started calling the hill, I was elected by default to go into Whiskey Springs for supplies.

One of my sisters had an infant and the other one had one on the way, so it was understandable that their husbands didn't want to leave them. Not one of them had a problem sending their brother into town.

Not that I minded getting out in the fresh air.

I whistled to myself as I made my way along the road leading to town. It was downhill all the way and uphill all the way back. I wasn't sure which was worse and I was pretty sure the horses didn't care for either.

But they were two good horses and didn't complain. One of them, in fact, was a war horse I'd bought off a fellow who'd fought in the war.

If the war had gone on for just one more year, I would have been in there. Like every other southern man worth his salt, fighting my way through a lost cause.

But fortunately or unfortunately, depending on which way the wind blew, the war had ended and I had come to Whiskey Springs with my four sisters.

Not only was I the middle child, I was the only boy out of five siblings. It was easy enough for a sane man to understand why I had been itching to join the army. I had still not ruled out joining the United States Cavalry.

I saw the girl standing there as I made my way around one of the switchbacks that made the trip downhill about a hundred percent safer, but I figured it was just a trick of the light.

The road between my sisters' houses and Whiskey Springs was deserted to say the least.

My brother-in-law, Graham, owned the whole mountain, so unless he had sold land to someone, this was all private property. I had it on good authority that that wasn't going to be happening anytime soon. Graham had every intention of passing along an unparalleled huge estate to his heirs.

Since his wife was already expecting her second child, he was obviously quite serious about that. He claimed that this land would increase exponentially in value over the next few hundred years.

Personally, I was more of a here and now kind of person. Since I had no heirs and no signs of any in my future, I didn't have to worry anyone other than myself.

About ninety percent of the time I was more than okay with that.

As I came around the curve, fully expecting the image of the young lady to have vanished, I saw her standing there looking quite vexed.

There were so many things wrong with this picture. First, she wasn't dressed properly for this kind of weather.

Second, she should not be out here alone. This country was still wild and there were men who would want to do her harm. My youngest sister, Elise, had gone through an encounter with such a man just last December, so I was more than aware of such things.

And third, she just looked so completely out of place. A woman standing on the edge of a mountain cliff with a stack of luggage looking completely lost.

I had four sisters. I knew when a girl was putting on a brave face.

I stopped the horses just as I reached her.

"Mind if I ask what you're doing out here?" I asked.

"Waiting for the…" She waved a hand in frustration. "Carriage to take me up to the house."

"The carriage—" Someone had sorely misled this girl. "Are you alone?"

She rolled her eyes at me. She was from the city, I decided. She had that sophisticated look about her. My sister, Bailey was going to love this lady's clothes. Bailey liked to keep up with the latest fashion.

"I'm Colton," I said. "I can take you up to the house."

"No," she said. "I'll just wait for the carriage."

Locking the wagon wheels, I climbed down and stood in front of her.

She had the most beautiful green eyes I had ever seen. With the late evening sunlight reflecting in her eyes, I saw little shards of dark green, light green, and the tiniest little gold sparkle.

Her heart-shaped face was classically perfect. And her bow-shaped lips begged to be kissed, even as she scowled at me.

"There is no carriage," I said.

"I was assured—"

I picked up one of her trunks and tossed it into the back of the wagon.

"Wait."

I picked up the other one and tossed it in back, too.

"What?" I asked. "You want to just stand out here for some mythical carriage? Sorry. I can't let you do it. You'll freeze to death. And there are wild animals."

She rubbed her arms and glanced around, her eyes wide now.

"I can walk," she said, but there was no conviction in her voice.

I took her big leather bag, put I over my own shoulder, then held out a hand to help her onto the wagon.

She just looked blankly at me.

This girl had no idea how to climb onto a wagon.

She screeched when I picked her up and set her unceremoniously on the wagon seat. She didn't weigh more than a sack of potatoes, but she smelled a whole lot better. Like a meadow of spring flowers.

"My hat," she said.

I looked down at her burgundy hat. Picked it up, dusted it off, and handed it to her.

I noticed, as I went around to get on the wagon, that she did not put it back on her head. She just held it in her lap.

"Where are we going?" she asked as we started moving forward.

"I have to turn this Titanic around," I said.

"Fine," she said, crossing her arms and staring straight ahead.

I grinned as I used a wide place in the trail to turn the horses and wagon around.

This woman had passion and grit. Something I'd had a hard time finding in any girl outside of family. She also had a hint of that southern accent that reminded me of home.

I was intrigued.

When I had us pointed in the right direction to go home, I took off my gloves and handed them her.

"Put these on," I said.

My sisters would have to do without their provisions for another day.

Keep Reading MOUNTBATTEN PINK...